WITHDRAWN

NATIVE AMERICAN FOLKLORE AND TRADITIONS

NATIVE AMERICAN FOLKLORE AND TRADITIONS

Edited by
ELSIE CLEWS
PARSONS

SIRIUS

SIRIUS

This edition published in 2019 by Sirius Publishing, a division of
Arcturus Publishing Limited,
26/27 Bickels Yard, 151–153 Bermondsey Street,
London SE1 3HA

ISBN: 978-1-78888-784-7
AD006524US

Printed in China

CONTENTS

INTRODUCTION

Both the fantastical legends and the everyday life of the first peoples of the Americas continue to fascinate us. Medicine men and shamans, potlatches and marriage ceremonies, harvests and hunts fill the pages to come. There are family feuds, ambitious men, poignant love stories, and powerful tales of the struggle to survive in a hostile climate. In these tales, we can recognise our own hopes and dreams as well as marvel at the diversity of traditions that have sprung up across North America

The stories range across the continent. They come from the Crow, the Blackfoot, the Menomini, the Iroquois, the Apache, the Mojave, the Nootka, and the Inuit (or Eskimos) respectively. The Crow and the Blackfoot roamed the Great Plains of Montana, Wyoming, the Dakotas, Saskatechwan, and Alberta. Semi-nomadic peoples, the horse and the buffalo became central to their way of life after the arrival of the Europeans. The Menomini and the Iroquois lived a more settled, agricultural existence along the shores of the Great Lakes and across much of the north-eastern United States. The Menomini were an Algonquin speaking people, one of the two major language groups of the region and fierce rivals of the Iroquois, who lived to the south and east of them. The Apache and the Mojave come from the southwestern plains of Arizona, Nevada, New Mexico and Colorado, and their long resistance to European incursion has established their reputation as fearsome warriors.

The Nootka, or Nuu-chah-nulth as they are now known, come from the west coast of Vancouver Island, where their impressive house posts and expressive potlatch ceremonies provide a very different culture from the inland peoples. And finally there are the Inuit, who live across the entire arctic region of the continent. The people in this tale come from Baffin Island to the north of Hudson's Bay, where temperatures rarely rise above freezing.

The stories within this volume were compiled by anthropologists aiming to bring the traditions of the Native Americans to a wider audience. Each writer did their best to discard their own biases and to present the tales as the truest possible representation of Native American life.

Fearing that the Native Americans were a "vanishing race," many sought to document the peoples and the culture before their traditional way of life was lost forever. As well as writing down the stories they heard, many Americans in the early 20th century sought to record the culture of the Native Americans for posterity through the new medium of photography.

There was no more renowned photographer than Edward Curtis. Curtis began working on his magnum opus, *The North American Indian*, in 1906 with the support of the businessman J. P. Morgan. Over the course of 20 years, he took more than 40,000 photographs of people from more than 80 different tribes. Along with the photographs themselves, he provided extensive annotations on the traditions, societies, and recreations of the peoples he saw through the lens of his camera. The portraits are a stunning tribute to the diversity of cultures in North America and help bring their stories to life.

Curtis is not the only artist featured in this collection—you will also find images from the photographers Joseph Dixon and Roland Reed, as well as paintings by accomplished artists such as Charles Marion Russell and Frederic Remington. The images range from the haunting to the joyful, from the alien to the familiar.

The tales here provide only a brief taste of Native American life. Both fascinating and entertaining, they give an insight into cultures that continue to endure more than a century after their predicted doom.

Takes-the-Pipe, A Crow Warrior

I

HORSES neighing, women scurrying to cover, the report of guns, his mother, Pretty-weasel, gashing her legs for mourning—that was Takes-the-pipe's earliest memory. Later he learned that his own father, a famous warrior of the Whistling-water clan, had fallen in the fight and that his "father", Deaf-bull, was really a paternal uncle who had married the widow. No real father could have been kinder than Deaf-bull. If anything, he seemed to prefer his brother's son to his own children, always petting him and favoring him with the choicest morsels.

When Pretty-weasel needed help in dressing a hide or pitching a tent, her sisters and cousins of the Sore-lip clan came as visitors, often bringing moccasins and gewgaws for their little clansman, Takes-the-pipe. One of the sisters stood out more clearly than the rest, a lusty wench who would pull Deaf-bull by the ear and pour water on his face when he took an afternoon nap. He in turn would throw her on the ground and tickle her till she bawled for mercy. Another salient figure was the grandmother, old Muskrat, who used to croon the boy to sleep with a lullaby: "The dog has eaten, he is smoking. Haha, huhu! Haha, huhu!" Whenever she came to the refrain she raised a wrinkled, mutilated hand, and snapped what remained of her fingers in the child's face.

The people were always traveling back and forth in those days. Now Takes-the-pipe was throwing stones into the Little Bighorn, then with other boys he was chasing moths in the Wolf Mountains. When he caught one he rubbed it against his breast, for they said that was the way to become a swift runner. One fall, the Mountain Crow traveled to the mouth of the Yellowstone to visit their kin of the River band. All

winter was spent there. It was fun coasting down-hill on a buffalo-rib toboggan and spinning tops on the smooth ice. Each boy tried to upset his neighbor's with his own, and when he succeeded he would cry, "I have knocked you out!" Takes-the-pipe was a good player, but once he came home inconsolable because his fine new top was stolen, and another time a bigger lad had cheated, "knocking him out" with a stone deftly substituted for the wooden toy. His mother comforted him saying, "That boy is crazy! His father is of the Bad-honors clan, that's why he acts that way!" Takes-the-pipe was still a little fellow when Deaf-bull made him a bow and arrows, and taught him to shoot. Now he ran about, letting fly his darts against birds and rabbits. There was ample chance to gain skill in archery. The boys would tie together a bundle of grass and set it on a knoll, then all shot at this target, and the winner took all his competitors' arrows. Whenever Takes-the-pipe brought home a sheaf of darts, his father would encourage him, saying, "You'll be like Sharp-horn, who always brings down his buffalo with the first shot." And when his son had killed his first cottontail, Deaf-bull proudly called Sliding-beaver, a renowned Whistling-water, feasted him royally and had him walk through camp, leading Takes-the-pipe mounted on his horse and proclaiming his success in a laudatory chant.

One spring there was great excitement. The supply of meat was exhausted, yet the buffalo remained out of sight. Scouts were sent to scour the country in search of game, but in vain. At last Sharp-horn offered to lure the buffalo by magic. At the foot of a cliff he had the men build a corral. He summoned Deaf-bull to be his assistant. "Bring me an old unbroken buffalo chip," he said. Takes-the-pipe found one, and together he and his father brought it to the shaman. "Someone is trying to starve us; my medicine is stronger than his; we will eat," said Sharp-horn. He smoothed the earth in his lodge and marked buffalo tracks all over. He put the chip on one of the tracks and on the chip a rock shaped like a buffalo's head, which he wore as a neck ornament. This rock he smeared with grease. "The buffalo are coming, bid the men drive them here," he said.

Deaf-bull went out and issued the orders received from Sharp-horn. On the heights above the corral, old men, women and children strung out in two diverging lines for the distance of a mile or two. The young men rode far out till they sighted the herd, got behind it and chased the game between the two lines nearer and nearer to the declivity. They drove them down into the corral. Some were killed in leaping, others stunned so they could be easily dispatched. That was a great day for Takes-the-pipe. He rode double with his father, and Deaf-bull was a person of consequence. Had he not assisted Sharp-horn? Then, too, he was a member of the Big Dog Society, and the Big Dogs were the police for that season with power to whip every man, woman or child who dared disobey Sharp-horn's orders.

After the hunt, the meat-racks sagged with the weight of the buffalo ribs, and the people made up for past want by gorging themselves with fat and tongues. One evening the Big Dogs held a feast and dance, the next evening the Fox society, then the Lumpwoods, and so on. There were promiscuous gatherings, too, where the valiant warriors rose to tell the assembled multitude about their exploits, while the old men exhorted the callow youths to emulate the example of their fathers and the camp reechoed the ancient warriors' songs:—

> Sky and earth are everlasting,
> Men must die.
> Old age is a thing of evil,
> Charge and die!

On one of these occasions Takes-the-pipe was proudly listening to Deaf-bull's record. He would have been a chief, had he ever wrested a gun from an enemy in a hand-to-hand encounter; in every other essential he more than passed muster. Three times he had crawled into a Piegan camp and stolen horses picketed to their owners' tents; six times he had "counted coup" on enemies, touching them with his lance or bare hand; twice he had carried the pipe and returned with blackened face as leader of a victorious expedition. While Takes-the-pipe was listening spell-bound to his father's narrative, he felt a sudden pinch. He turned round to smite his tormentor only to face Cherry-necklace, a boy somewhat older than himself. He was Sliding-beaver's son and that put a different complexion on the matter, for Sliding-beaver, like Deaf-bull, was a Whistling-water, so their sons might take what liberties they chose with each other and enjoy complete immunity. At present, however, Cherry-necklace had more important business than playing

a trick on Takes-the-pipe. "Magpie," he whispered, "they are playing magpie." Off both boys dashed to a creek nearby, where some twenty lads were already assembled round a big fire. They smeared their faces with charcoal till one could hardly recognize his neighbor. "Now, we'll be magpies," they said, "Takes-the-pipe is a swift runner, he shall lead." They scampered back to camp. The women, seeing them approach in their disguise, snatched their meat from the racks to hide it inside their tents. But Takes-the-pipe had already fixed his eye on some prime ribs, pounced upon them and carried off his prize, followed by the other boys, each vanishing with what booty he could safely capture.

It was a great gathering about the fireplace by the stream. One of the lads strutted up and down as a crier and announced, "Takes-the-pipe has stolen the best piece!" Then he and a few others who had won like delicacies were granted their choice of the spoils, whereupon all feasted. When they had done eating, the oldest boy declared, "We'll remain seated here. If anyone gets up, we'll rub our hands with this grease and smear it over his body." So they sat still for a long time. At last Cherry-necklace forgot about the warning and got up. In an instant they were upon him like a pack of wolves. Here was a fine chance for Takes-the-pipe to get even for that pinch; he daubed Cherry-necklace's face all over with the fat. Others followed suit and soon his body glistened with grease. He leaped into the creek to wash it off, but the water glided off the fat.

II

The people were moving along the Bighorn, with the long lodge poles dragging along the ground. Some dozen girls with toy tents were transporting them in imitation of their mothers. Takes-the-pipe was riding with the Hammers, a boys' club patterned on the men's societies. The members treated dogs or deer as enemies and practised counting coup on them. Takes-the-pipe as one of the dare-devils carried one of the emblems of the organization, a long stick with a wooden hammer-head pivoted some two feet from its top. Suddenly an idea struck him. "Hammers," he cried, "let us offer a seat on our horses to the girls we like!" No sooner said than done. He himself had had his eye on Otter for some time, and presently the two were riding double.

In the evening when the women of the camp pitched their lodges, the Hammer boys' sweethearts set up theirs a little way off. They played at married life. Takes-the-pipe sneaked into his mother's lodge, purloined some meat, brought it near Otter's tent, and bade her fetch the food, which she then cooked for him. Other boys and girls did likewise. Thus they played every day while on the march. Once Takes-the-pipe killed a young wolf and brought a lock of its hair to the young folks' camp. He pretended that it was an enemy's scalp and set it on a pole and all the girls had to dance the scalp dance around it. There followed a recital of deeds; the boys who had struck wolves were allowed to claim coups against the Dakota, and those who had touched deer might boast of having stolen picketed horses.

It was a gay journey. But one evening when Takes-the-pipe had bragged of his mock exploits, Cherry-necklace suddenly appeared on the scene and taunted him before all his playmates, "You think you are a man, because you are as tall as Deaf-bull," he cried, "you are nothing but a child fit to play with little girls. Have you ever been on the war-path? I went with Long-horse and struck a Piegan." Takes-the-pipe hung his head. It was only too true. Cherry-necklace was not so much older, yet he had already distinguished himself and might recite his coup in any public assembly. Takes-the-pipe had no answer for he knew nothing to fling back in his "joking-relative's" teeth, but he resolved forthwith to join a war party at the earliest opportunity.

Not long after this Shinbone let it be known that he was setting out on a horse-raid against the Dakota. Now Takes-the-pipe had his chance. Well-provided with moccasins by his clanswomen, he joined a dozen young men starting afoot on the perilous adventure—perilous because, though Shinbone was a brave man, this was his first attempt at leading a party and it remained to be seen whether "his medicine was good." They walked for four days. As Takes-the pipe was the youngest of the company, he had to fetch water and firewood, and one morning when he slept too late they poured water all over him.

Warily the party advanced. On the fourth evening Shinbone ordered them to halt on a little knoll. "Yonder are the Dakota lodges," he said, "early to-morrow morning we will go there." He took his sacred bundle, unwrapping a weasel skin stuffed with deer hair, and pointed it toward the camp. "The Dakota are tired," he said, "they will sleep late." Before

dawn he roused the party. He appointed two young men as scouts. They came back. "Well," he asked, "how is it?"

"Where you pointed, there are the Dakota lodges," they replied. "It is well," he said. He chose four others to drive all the loose horses out of the camp. They left. They had not gone far when they were overtaken by Takes-the-pipe. "What are you doing? Go back. He did not send you."

"I am going to the camp to cut a horse or strike a coup."

"You are crazy! We are older than you and are still without honors. We are here to steal horses, not to score deeds. The one who is carrying our pipe is a new leader, he may not be very powerful and you will spoil his luck. Go back!"

But though they threatened to beat him, Takes-the-pipe would not return and so all five approached the camp. There were the lodges ranged in a circle. The inmates seemed plunged in sleep. Near the edge a herd of horses were peacefully grazing. The scouts quietly stole up to them and began to drive them off toward the rest of their party. In the meantime Takes-the-pipe was getting his bearings in the strange encampment. He cast about for a picketed horse, but there was none to be seen. Then of a sudden, chance favored him. Out of a little tent on the outskirts of the circle a wizened old man came hobbling on a staff. Takes-the-pipe stole up behind him and dealt him a stunning blow. "Heha!" he cried, counting coup on the prostrate foe. Then he dashed towards his friends, who had watched him from a little distance. As yet there was no alarm, but no time was to be lost. They mounted and drove the horses before them. When they reached Shinbone, the rest of the party got on horseback. "Now we will run!" said the captain.

They had come and gone to the Dakota afoot and slowly enough; now they were mounted, and traveled at top speed, for they knew that before long the enemy would be in their wake. They rode on and on till they got to the brink of a rapid stream. Here, some of their stolen horses turned back, but the greatest number they saved, driving them through the ice-cold water, where they themselves felt as though they must die from the cold. They traveled that day and all through the night without stopping to eat. On the following morning they reached the Crow camp, sore and worn out, but with sixty head of horses. By rights they all belonged to Shinbone, but after the fashion of a good leader, he was generous to his followers and let them have nearly half of the herd. Takes-the-pipe won three horses. His parents rejoiced when they heard of his coup and his booty. His mother and her sisters at once prepared a magnificent feast, to which all the Sore-lip women contributed. On such occasions it behooved a young man to give lavish entertainment to his father's kin, so that he might live to be an old man. So Deaf-bull invited all the eminent Whistling-water men, and Takes-the-pipe selected Sliding-beaver from among them, presenting him with a fine bay horse. Then Sliding-beaver trudged through camp, leading Takes the-pipe's horse and singing the young man's praises.

III

He was rolling a hoop and another youth was hurling a dart at it when Shinbone clutched him by the arm. "Come, I'll make a man of you. You shall take the place of your elder brother." Takes-the-pipe knew what he meant: a cousin of his belonging to the Fox society had fallen in a skirmish with the Dakota, and his fellow-members had been casting about for a clubbable kinsman. Now a new sort of life began for Takes-the-pipe. He no longer roamed about aimlessly or consorted with random companions. His fellow-members were now his constant associates. Spare time was whiled away in the lodges of eminent Foxes, beating the drum and singing the songs of the organization. Now and then the younger members took jaunts to the hills with their sweethearts. Again there was a philandering when the Foxes and their girls went berrying or up to the mountains to drag lodge poles to camp. Often enough a wealthy member had a herald invite all the Foxes to his lodges, where they were feasted, and held a dance. There, too, valiant men rose to expatiate on their prowess. The Foxes had done well that year. Shinbone had struck the first coup of the season, thus making his club take precedence of the rival Lumpwood society. By the rules of the game the Lumpwoods had lost the right to sing their own songs, and when they danced they were obliged to borrow those of the Big Dogs, exposing themselves to the mockery of the Foxes. That year Takes-the-pipe joined a number of war parties and succeeded in capturing an enemy's gun. Now he, too, would rise and tell about his martial experiences.

The following spring there were great doings. The Foxes were electing new officers in place of the last year's standard-bearers. Three or four of the elders had had a council and now they came to the club lodge where all the members were gathered. Two of the emblems of the society were straight staffs, two were hooked and wrapped with otterskin. Each was pointed at the bottom, for in sight of the enemy the bearer was obliged to plant it into the earth, and stand his ground regardless of danger or death, without budging an inch unless a companion plucked out the fatal lance. That was why the officers were called "men doomed to die." If they escaped unscathed by the end of the year, they retired with all the honors of distinguished service; if they died in battle, they were solemnly mourned by their fellow-members and other tribes men; but if they failed in duty, they became the pariahs of the camp. There were not many young men eager to undertake so arduous an office. The electors were passing round the circle, offering a pipe to likely candidates, for to smoke it meant acceptance. Some of the faint-hearted ones crouched behind others to escape notice and even some, who were forward enough on other occasions, shrank back. First the elders went to the tried warriors. No trouble was expected with Shinbone, and as a matter of fact he readily consented. Next they came to Lone-pine, Sliding-beaver's eldest son. He, too, smoked without sign of reluctance. But now the electors were beginning to cast about among the younger fellow-members, for they were coming towards Cherry-necklace. Cherry-necklace was no coward; he had shown his mettle in more than one encounter. Yet he was very fond of having a good time. Would he willingly accept appointment? No, he was squirming uneasily and refused the pipe. Rather, he would have refused it, but Lone-pine, his brother, seized him by the bang of his hair and forcibly made his lips touch the pipestem. Thus Cherry-necklace too was "doomed to die." And now the elders passed round once more in search of the last officer. Takes-the-pipe's heart began to beat. What if they asked him? It would be an honor for one so young, but did he wish to die? They were coming straight toward him. He seemed to hear the old song:

> Sky and earth are everlasting,
> Men must die.

Yes, if he died, what mattered it? He would yield without coaxing and shame Cherry-necklace. He eagerly clutched the pipe and became one of the bearers of a hooked-staff.

While the Foxes were holding their annual election, the Lumpwoods were going through a like procedure. A day or two later, a defiant call was heard from their lodge. They were ready for the annual indulgence in licensed wife-stealing. Only the Foxes and the Lumpwoods took part in this pastime, the other societies being mere spectators. If a Fox had ever had for his sweetheart a Lumpwood's wife, he was now privileged to kidnap her from her rightful husband, who would only make himself a laughing-stock if he interposed objections, let alone violence. Takes-the-pipe remembered that Otter was now married to a Lumpwood named Drags-the-wolf, so he went to the lodge and called her.

NE-SOT-A-QUOIT

A FOX CHIEF

Philadelphia Published by F. C. Biddle

Drags-the-wolf was game. He had the reputation of being very fond of his pretty, young wife, but he knew the proper way for a Crow to act. Instead of restraining her, he himself said, "He is calling you. Go!" Takes-the-pipe brought her to his parents' lodge. His mother and sisters gave her a beautiful elk-tooth dress and other Sore-lip women from all over the camp brought her moccasins and beaded pouches. Then the Foxes selected from their number an old man who had once rescued a wounded tribesman from certain death by dashing into the thick of the fray, and carrying him off on his horse. This man, for none other might venture, rode double with the kidnapped bride, all the other Foxes parading jubilantly behind and twitting their rivals with the capture of so handsome a Lumpwood woman.

IV

Shinbone had come home from a war party with blackened face and taken the rank of chief. No wonder, the people were saying. Had not the Thunderbird adopted him when as a young man he prayed and thirsted for a revelation? Men must undergo suffering if they wanted supernatural blessing so that they could become great men among their people. Of all the Crow chiefs, only Drags-the-wolf had been in luck: him the Moon visited as he was peacefully slumbering in his tent and granted him invulnerability and coups. The other distinguished warriors had had to mortify their flesh in order to gain favor.

That spring the herald proclaimed that Red-eye was going to hold a Sun Dance. He had lost a brother and was hungering for revenge. What surer way to attain it than to fast and dance before the sacred doll till it became alive and showed him a scalped Dakota in earnest of victory and vengeance? But Red-eye's announcement was a signal for all the ambitious youths to plan for a public mortification of their flesh at the same time in the hope of winning supernatural favor. So, while the pledger of the ceremony was dancing up and down with his gaze riveted on the holy image in the rear of the lodge, a dozen young men were undergoing torture for their own ends. Some were dragging through camp two buffalo skulls fastened to a stick thrust through holes cut in their backs. Others—and Takes-the-pipe among them—decided to swing from the lodge poles. So he begged Sharp-horn to pierce the flesh above his breasts, run skewers through the openings, and tie the rods to ropes hung from a pole. Thus attached he ran back and forth till he had torn out the skewers. Yet when he had fallen to the ground faint and blood stained no vision came for all his pains.

He wanted to become a chief like Shinbone, so he went on a mountain peak to fast. Without clothes save his gee-string and a buffalo robe, he slept there overnight. He awoke early, the sun had just risen. He took a piece of wood and put on it his left forefinger. "Sun," he cried, "I am miserable. I am giving you this. Make me a chief!" With a huge knife he hacked off the first joint. The blood began to flow. He lost consciousness. When he came to, it was evening. His finger ached. He tried to sleep, but the pain and cold kept him awake. Of a sudden he heard a man clearing his throat and a horse's neighing came closer and closer. A voice behind him said, "The one whom you wanted to come has arrived." He turned about. He saw a man on a bay horse; his face was painted red and he wore a shirt with many discs cut out from its body, yet hanging from it as though by a thread. From the back of his head rose a chicken-hawk feather. The rider said, "You are miserable. I have been looking for you for a long time but could never quite reach you. I will adopt you as my child. Look! I am going to run." He began to gallop; the dust flew to the sky. Then the trees and shrubs all about turned into Piegans and began shooting at the horseman. Arrows came whizzing by him and bullets flew round him and the enemies were yelling after him, but he wheeled round unscathed. With his spear he knocked down one warrior and counted coup on him. He rode up to Takes-the-pipe: "Though you fight all the people of the world, dress as I do and you need have no fear of death before you are a chief. That man I struck is a Piegan; you have seen his country, go there, I give him to you. As I am, so shall you be; arrows will not hurt you, bullets you can laugh at. You shall be like a rock. But one thing you must not do: never eat of any animal's kidneys."

When Takes-the-pipe got back to his people, he was very glad.

Two things remained to be done before he might call himself chief: one was to lead a victorious war party, the other to cut a picketed horse. His vision enabled him forthwith to play a captain's part. He shot a chicken-hawk and took one of its feathers to be worn at the back of his head on his expeditions. He prepared a shirt like the one he had seen and a spear that resembled exactly that borne by his patron. Then he gathered his war party. His sisters and other Sore-lip women made moccasins galore for him. He set out in the dead of night. For several days they traveled north and west. On the Missouri they ran into a few Piegans in a hunting lodge. They killed them all and took their scalps. Thus they could return with blackened faces. One of the enemies had a thumbless hand, so the year was known ever after as "the winter when they killed the thumbless man."

V

He had been wounded in the knee. He could not understand it. He had been promised that his body would be like stone. He had worn his feather at the back of his head, as in every fight since the time of his vision, yet his kneecap had been shattered in a skirmish with the Dakota. And it was an ugly injury. Red-eye had salved it with bear root, but the cure-all had failed. Bullsnake, foremost of doctors, blessed by the buffalo, had waded into the river to wash his knee, but all in vain; he remained crippled. Then he knew that he had unwittingly broken his guardian spirit's rule; there had been a feast before the fatal battle and then he must have eaten of the forbidden food.

Soon there came surety. In a dream appeared the man on the bay horse and said: "I told you not to eat kidney, you have eaten it. You shall never be chief." Takes-the-pipe had now struck many coups and captured guns and carried the captain's pipe. His record surpassed that of any man of his age, but he lacked the honor of cutting a picketed horse. How could he ever gain it now? Horse raiders started on foot, and he could only painfully limp across the camp.

Young women, drawn by his fame, often visited him in his tent, but their attentions soon palled on him. His mother tried to console him. "Of all the young men you are the best-off; you have struck more coups than the rest and own plenty of horses; the young women are crazy about you. You ought to be the happiest man in camp." But he would watch the bustle of preparations for new raids that he could not join; he would ride about of an evening and chance upon the foot-soldiers setting out from their trysting-place, and would look after them, wistful and envious and

sick at heart. Sharp-horn, the aged sage, advised him to go for another vision; possibly the guardian spirit would relent. So Takes-the-pipe started out on horseback and rode far away towards the mountain where he had prayed before. At the foot he hobbled his horse and painfully climbed to the summit. He lay down, with outstretched arms, facing the sky. "Father," he wailed, "I am miserable, take pity on me." He lay there during the night but at the first glimmer of dawn there was still no message from the mysterious powers. All day he stayed about the jagged bowlders without drink or a morsel to eat. Long after nightfall a muffled tread became audible and as it came closer it was the tramp of a buffalo. Then a bull was standing over him, scenting his breath and caressing his naked breast with shaggy fur. At last he spoke in Crow. "I will adopt you my son. I have seen you suffering from afar. What other Indians have prayed for shall be yours. Look at the inside of my mouth." He looked and there was not a tooth to be seen. "So long as you have teeth, my son, you shall not die. You shall marry a fine, chaste, young woman and beget children and see your grandchildren about you. When you die you shall be so old that your skin will crack as you move from one corner of the lodge to another."

But Takes-the-pipe shook his head and said, "Father, it is not because I crave old age that I am thirsting; I want to be a chief like Shinbone."

"My son, what you ask is difficult. As I hurried to you from my home, I overtook another person traveling towards you; perhaps you will still be able to get what you desire." Takes-the-pipe sat up to ask further counsel, but the bull was gone and nothing but a bleached buffalo skull was gaping at him in the gloaming. All next day he fasted and prayed on his peak, addressing now the Sun, then the Thunder, then again the Morningstar. His throat was parched when he lay down at dark in his old resting-place. He did not know how, but of a sudden the darkness was lifted and the hilltop shone with a gentle radiance. An old woman was standing at his feet, resting on a digging-stick; she wore a splendid robe with horsetracks marked on it in porcupine-quill embroidery. "My child," she said, "you have not called me, nevertheless I am here. I heard your groans and started towards you but another person passed me on the road. I am the Moon. When children fall sick, doctor them with this root; their parents will give you horses. I will make you the wealthiest of all the Crows."

But Takes-the-pipe shook his head and answered, "Grandmother, I am not suffering to gain wealth, I want to become a chief like Shinbone."

"My dear child, you are asking for something great. As I came hither, I saw another person starting to come here. Perhaps he has more power than I, and can grant your wish." He was eager to ask her more, but her form faded into nothing and only the sheen of the waning crescent remained visible.

Another day he fasted and drank no water. He was now very weak, so that he dragged himself about with the aid of a cane. Was there no power to help him in his distress? Night came as he lay wailing and peering into the darkness, when a handsome young man stood before him. "I was sleeping far away, you have roused me with your lamentations," he said. "I have come to help you. You shall be my son. Do you recognize me? I am the Tobacco your old people plant every year. So long as they harvest me, the Crow shall be a great tribe. They have forgotten the way to prepare the seed, their crops will be poor. I will show you how to mix it before planting. Then you will make your tribe great and teach others and receive all sorts of property in payment."

And Takes-the-pipe answered; "Father, I am not suffering in order to plant tobacco and gain property, I want to be a chief like Shinbone."

Then the man replied, "My son, everything else in the universe is easy for me, only what you ask for is hard. That one who used to be your father is very strong. 'Don't eat kidney,' he said. You have eaten it. I cannot make you chief. Listen, my son. All things in the world go by fours. Three of us have come to help you. We have been powerless. A fourth one is coming, perhaps he can do it."

The next day Takes-the-pipe could hardly crawl on all-fours. His head swam. He seized his knife and chopped off another finger joint on his left hand. Then holding aloft the bleeding stump he cried, "Fathers, I am giving you this. Make me a chief!" Suddenly a huge figure came panting toward him, shaking a rattle and singing a song. "I am the last," said a big bear; "though I am heavy and slow, I have arrived."

Takes-the-pipe called out to him joyfully, "Father, I knew you were coming. Cure my knee so that I can go out to cut a picketed horse and become a chief."

"My son, the one who used to be your father is very strong. He does not want you to be a chief. Well, I too am strong. If you are a man, I can

help you. If you are faint-hearted, I am powerless." "Father," said Takes-the-pipe, "make me great; make me greater than other men, and if I die what matters it?"

"My son, there are many chiefs in camp; of your kind there shall be but one. Tell me, have you ever seen the whole world?" Without waiting for an answer, the bear lifted him up. Mountains and streams and prairies and camps came into his vision. The berries were ripe and the Crow camp loomed in sight and the Tobacco society were harvesting the precious seed. Far away were hostile lodges. Then the leaves were turning yellow and the enemy were setting out to raid Crow horses. One Crow all alone was riding towards them. "My son, do you see that horseman with trailing sashes? They were trying to hold him back, he has broken loose. He could not be a chief; he wants to die. He is a Crazy Dog. He speaks 'backward'; he cares little for the rules of the camp. Where there is danger, he is the foremost. Dress like him, act like him, and you shall be great. The people will speak of you so long as there are Crows living on this earth. This I will give you if your heart is strong."

"Thanks, father, thanks! What you have shown me is great; I will do it. I wanted to live and be a chief. It cannot be. There is no way for me to live; I shall die as a Crazy Dog."

Then the bear vanished.

VI

The people were gathered near the mouth of the Bighorn. There was merriment in camp after a successful hunt. Suddenly was heard the beating of a drum and the chanting of a strange song. All ran out of their lodges to see what was going on. Who is that man on the richly fitted-out horse? He approaches the center of the circle, shaking a rattle. Two sashes of deerskin, slipped over his head, descend to the ground. Sliding-beaver is leading the horse, halting from time to time, and beating a drum. At the fourth stop he cried aloud: "Young women, if you would be this man's sweethearts, you must hasten, he is about to die!" Then he beat his drum and addressed the rider: "Remain on horseback, do not dance!"

Forthwith Takes-the-pipe dismounted and danced in position. Then because he did the opposite of what he was told everyone knew him for a Crazy Dog pledged to court death. Straightway Pretty-weasel began to lament: "I begged him not to do it; he has done it!" But the other women cheered lustily, and Sliding-beaver sang his praises aloud as he slowly led him outside of the camp circle. Then for a while he appeared every evening, dancing and shaking his rattle. He would ride through camp like a madman. When a few were gathered eating some meat, he would walk his horse into their very midst as if to run over them. Then they would cry out, "Trample on us." And the Crazy Dog would turn aside and let them eat in peace. At night the best-looking young women paid him visits; even married women went there and their husbands did not mind it. Sometimes two or three would come of a single night. Famous Whistling-waters came to tell him what a great thing he was doing. All the eminent warriors in camp, Drags-the-wolf, Red-eye, and Shinbone, were looking on him with envy. The cherries had ripened and one day a woman offered him some. He said, "When I decided to do this, the grass was sprouting. I did not expect to live so long, yet to-day I am eating cherries. Well, I will see whether I can achieve what I wish." When they went hunting the next time, he got some buffalo blood and mixed it with badger blood and water. In the mixture he saw his image with blood streaming down his face. "Yes," he cried, "I have seen it. What I am longing for is coming true!"

The leaves were turning yellow when a tribesman caught sight of some Dakota raiders. The young men drove them off and the enemy took refuge in the dry bed of a stream. There, the Crow warriors were going to attack them. They were getting ready when Pretty-weasel rushed into their midst, crying, "Bind my son! Don't let him go!" They looked for him. He was not to be found. All alone he was dashing to-ward the enemy. They galloped after him. He was close to the coulee, shaking his rattle and singing his song:—

> Sky and earth are everlasting,
> Men must die.
> Old age is a thing of evil,
> Charge and die!

He rode straight up to the enemies' hiding-place. At the edge he dismounted. Several Dakotas were peeping out. "There is no way for me to live," he cried, "I must die!" He shot one foe and struck him with his rattle. Then another Dakota shot him in the left temple, and Takes-the-pipe fell dead.

The Crow warriors caught up, and killed every man in the raiding party. Pretty-weasel reached the spot and wiped the blood from her son's forehead. The men put him on a horse and brought him to camp. Wailing, they went home. There the Sore-lip women clipped their hair and gashed their legs. The Whistling-water men rode up and down singing the praises of the dead Crazy Dog. His fellow-Foxes propped up the corpse against a backrest, knelt before it and wailed. Their officers ran arrows through their flesh and jabbed their foreheads till the blood flowed in streams. Then they set up a scaffold on four posts, wrapped the body in a robe, and placed it on top. Beside the stage they planted a pole. From it was hung his drum, and his sashes swept down as streamers blowing in the wind. His rattle they put into his hand. Then the camp moved.

Robert H. Lowie

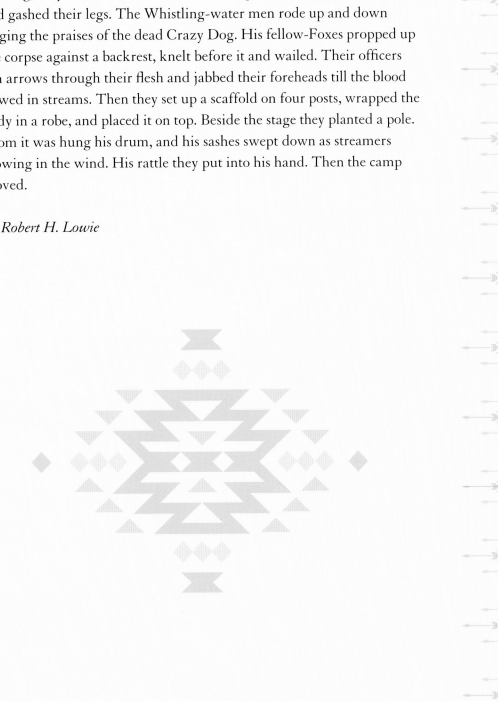

A TRIAL OF SHAMANS

BIG-DOG was troubled; he knew he should not sleep that night. White-hip, blind old White-hip, had passed him with a taunt. He did not mind the old fellow's gibes, yet....

It all happened long ago. White-hip was stretched out in his lodge one night when a young kinsman named Shows-his-horse burst in upon him.

"They say you are a great medicine man, take pity on me, I am in distress."

"Well, what ails you?"

"As I approached my tent this evening, a man came out, wrapped in his robe. He has stolen my wife; I want revenge."

Then White-hip said, "You are my younger brother; I will help you. Who is it that has stolen your wife?"

Shows-his-horse replied, "It was Big-dog."

Then White-hip shrank back and asked, "Are you sure it was Big-dog? The night is dark, you may have made a mistake."

But the young man answered, "It was still light when I saw him,—a short, stocky man with the wolf-tails at his heels plainly visible dragging along the ground."

White-hip said, "My younger brother, it is wrong for a man to mind the loss of a woman. If your joking-relatives should hear of this, they will sing songs in mockery of you. This is dangerous business. The Thunder himself has adopted Big-dog as his child."

Then Shows-his-horse flared up. "They told me you were a great medicine man, that is why I came to you in my grief. I see you are afraid; your medicine is worthless."

Then for a long time White-hip spoke not a word. At length he said, "It will be very difficult, but my medicine is strong. Though the Thunder himself be his father, I will lay him low."

It happened that a few days later Big-dog set out on a war party against the Sioux. Then White-hip prayed to the sacred stone that was his medicine. And Big-dog's war party was met by a superior force of Sioux that killed one of his followers and scattered the rest. There was grief in the Crow camp and the people were wondering about Big-dog's first failure. But Shows-his-horse brought his three best horses as a gift to White-hip, and slowly the news leaked out that a trial of strength was on between the two great shamans of the tribe.

Soon after this event White-hip, too, wanted to go on the warpath, and the men who had been thwarted by Big-dog's failure were eager to join him. But the very night they set out, Big-dog prayed to the Thunder: "I do not want you to afflict my people; only he that leads them shall meet with disaster." And it rained and stormed in the war party's path, and a tree, felled by lightening, grazed the captain's shoulder. Then the braves were alarmed and insisted on turning back.

Thus, when either of the shamans had set out against the enemy, the other was sure to thwart him, till neither ventured on a war party, and the whole camp were wondering who should conquer in the end. At last Big-dog could contain himself no longer. Once more he addressed the Thunder: "These scars are from the flesh I cut as an offering to you, these finger-joints were chopped to make you a present. You made me your child. That one is mocking me and you. He thinks his is the greater medicine; smite him with blindness."

And before the cherries had ripened, White-hip had lost his sight. Then Big-dog triumphed and the Crows all said that he was the greatest shaman they had ever had and that his medicine was the most powerful of all; and White-hip was deserted by all but his next of kin, and became so poor that for a while a rope served him for a belt.

But the blind man still had faith in his medicine and one day he thus invoked it: "His father has made me blind and miserable. I do not care if you can make him miserable too. He has three sons. Kill them all and make him live till his skin cracks from old age and force him to beg his food from strangers."

Then on the next war party Big-dog's eldest son was slain by the Blackfoot; and people began to say that perhaps White-hip had not been conquered for good. And a year later his second eldest son died from sickness. Then the Crows all said it must be White-hip's work. And before the leaves had turned yellow, the shaman's last son was drowned in the Yellowstone. Then some said that, for all that, Big-dog had won, for he himself was well, while his enemy was blind. But others thought that White-hip, despite his blindness, had shown himself superior.

And as years passed, Big-dog grew infirm. He outlived his nearest kin and those more remote till no clansfolk remained. He would wander about from lodge to lodge, feasting on what strangers offered him in sheer compassion. He would hear mothers whispering to their children, "Big-dog was a great medicine man once and the whole tribe stood in awe of him, but White-hip had the greater medicine and laid him low."

And just now White-hip had passed him with a taunt. He did not mind the blind fellow's mockery, but one thought troubled and racked him and would not let him sleep at night: "Whose medicine was really the greater? Who had won?"

Robert H. Lowie

Smoking-star, a Blackfoot Shaman

It was one evening in summer, the time of the long day, when the twilight is equally long, that I sat before the tepee fire of my host, Smoking-star. According to his own belief, he had seen the snows of nine times around his hands, or ninety years, as we count it. He was regarded as by far the oldest living Blackfoot, but his eye was bright and his memory good. That evening as we smoked in silence, I mused on the cross-section of man's history this venerable life would reveal, if it could be read. I told him how I felt, and my pleasure if he would tell his story for me. He sat long and silently, as is the way of his people; then rose, and with great dignity, left the tepee. Presently he returned and when seated, said, "The Smoking-star, Mars, is high. He shines approvingly. I have long lived by his power. I believe He will not be offended if I tell you the story of my life."

So runs the tale of old Smoking-star as near as my memory can follow :

My father's name was Old-beaver, chief of the Small-robe band, to which band I still belong. My mother came from the Fat-roasting band, she was the younger wife of my father, her older sister being the first, or head-wife. A child always calls each of his father's women mother and also all the women married to father's and mother's brothers; just why this is we do not know, but it is our way. My father was very kind to me, but my older mother was cross.

I suppose I was born in a small tepee set up outside, for such is the custom. Also I suppose that for a time my mother laid aside all ornaments and affected carelessness of person. If anyone should gaze at her, she would say, "Don't. My child will look like you; you are ugly, etc." She was attended by women only, for men should not approach the birthplace. Even my father was not permitted to enter and it was many days before he saw me. In due time, I suppose, I was strapped to a cradle

board. Later, a name was conferred upon me by my father, he being a chief. Unless a man is great, he does not name his child, but calls some man possessing these qualifications. Having once captured two guns from the Cree, my father told the story of that deed, or coup, and named me Two-guns. It is the belief that the qualities of the namer and the name itself pass to the child; hence great importance is given to the name and the conferring of it is a solemn occasion. The blackrobe (priest) tells me it is much the same with your people.

Also, I suppose that when I got my first tooth, my grandmothers reminded my parents that it was time to do something. So a feast was made, presents given, and prayers offered. This was, no doubt, repeated when I took my first step and when I learned to speak. But I do remember having my ears pierced. That is the first memory of childhood. I can still see a terrible looking old grandmother standing up before me, holding up a bone awl. I was never so frightened in my life. You have seen how it is done at the sun dance, where some old woman cries out, "I quilled a robe, all with these hands. So I have the power to do this." Just like a warrior recounting a coup.

My real mother never reproved me, but when I began to run about, my older mother did not like to have me meddling with her things. Often she would make threats to me in a kind of song, as—"There is a coyote outside. Come coyote, and eat up this naughty baby." Again, "Come old Crooked-back woman; bring your meat pounder; smash this baby's head." The woman referred to was a crazy cripple who terrorized the children because some of them teased her. I was very much afraid, so that usually all my older mother need say was, "Sh-h-h!" and mumble something about the coyote or the woman. I have noticed that among your people, parents strike their children. That is not our way. If they will not listen to advice, an uncle may be called upon to exercise discipline and if necessary he will punish, but whipping is the way of the police societies. Once I saw the police whip a chief because he broke the rules of the buffalo hunt.

Soon I began to play with the older boys; in winter we spun tops on the ice and in the snow, coasted the hills on toboggans made of buffalo ribs, or just stood up on a dry skin, holding up the end. In summer there were all kinds of games: racing, follow-the-leader, arrow games, the wheel game, etc. I had a hobby-horse, made of a bent stick, with a saddle and bridle, upon which I played running buffalo and going to war. I even learned to play tricks upon old people. Sometimes we would be playing where old women came to gather firewood and when one of them had a great heap of wood on her pack line, she would squat with her back against the wood, the lines in her hands, and call for us to help raise the load; occasionally, we would assist until she reached her feet and then, with a quick push, send her sprawling with the wood on top. Then we would run away to escape a beating.

Again, as water was carried in pails made of buffalo paunch, some boys would ambush the path and shoot an arrow into the pail, letting out the water. But usually we let older people alone, for, if caught, we were severely handled. When about six years old one of my grandfathers made me a bow; he prayed for me and said if I killed anything I should bring in the scalp to prove it. He told me the story of Scar-face and the dangerous birds. Some time after this I killed a bird, my first, and my father made a feast, calling in many great men, who smoked many pipes, told of great deeds and predicted that I would be a great warrior. The skin of the bird was put into my grandfather's war bundle.

When we traveled my mother carried me on her saddle or put me on a travois, hitched to a dog or some trusty old mare. But when I was old enough to ride alone, my father went on the war path to the Assiniboin country and brought back six horses; one pony he gave to me. Before I learned to ride it well, it was stolen by the Cree. At the same time my older mother was killed and scalped while out picking berries. All this made a deep impression upon me and I resolved to prepare for the war-path and to take vengeance on the Cree, particularly for the loss of my pony. In the meantime my father gave me another pony.

One morning when I was about eleven years old, I was terribly frightened to find a man from a police society standing at the door, shouting for me to come out at once. It was cold and stormy, but he ordered me to the water for a plunge and when I stood on the bank whimpering, he threw me headlong into the icy current. The older boys were splashing about gaily, but it was hard for me. When I crept back to the tepee, shivering, my old grandmother began to sing a derisive song about a would-be warrior who turned to an old woman. After that I went daily to the bath and soon became hard and strong.

The next summer our people were camped on Milk River where buffalo were plenty. The berries were just turning. One day while herding the horses I fell to eating berries and that night became ill. The next day I was very sick and a doctor was sent for. Old One-ear came, a man all of us feared, sat by my bed, beat upon a drum, sang in a loud voice, then turned down the robes that covered me, held a tube of bone against my breast and sucked violently. Then he arose and spat out a grasshopper. Everyone said that I would soon be well, and I was. But while I was too weak to go out, my grandfather came in and told me tales of the war-path and occasionally of the Lost Children, the Woman-who-went-to-the-sky, Morningstar, Scar-face, Blood-clot, and other tales. I came to take a deep interest in these tales and to think more and more of going to war. When I could go out, my people were holding the sun dance and one evening I heard my father reciting his coups, putting on the fire a stick for each. At last when there was a great blaze from so much wood, the people all shouted. It was a proud moment for me and from then on I began to train for the war-path.

Before cold weather our people separated, as was their custom, and our band, with the Fat-roasters and the Many-medicines, made winter camp on the Two Medicine River. It was a cold winter, but buffalo were plenty and we did not mind. In the spring my father led a war party against the Crow. I knew nothing of it until they had gone, but even had I known, he would not have taken me. I felt very sad and spent most of the time sitting on a hill, meditating. One day, on coming to camp I heard the women and even old men wailing. I saw my mother before our door hacking her bare leg with her butchering knife. Then I knew what had happened. The camp crier began to shout out that a runner had come in from a distant camp to say that Old-beaver and all his party had been killed by the Crows. When I met my old grandmother, with blood streaming down her bare arms, the sight sickened me and I fled to the hilltop and meditated further. As I thought of how coup had been counted on my father, my anger grew and I vowed to take a Crow scalp at the first opportunity.

Our camp mourned long after this. It was also necessary to select a new chief. One Good-runner was well thought of and was our choice, but an evil-minded fellow named Crow-eye sought the place. Finding that he was in disfavor, Crow-eye secretly loaded a gun, entered the tepee of Good-runner and shot him down. Crow-eye's relatives put him on a horse and sent him away for a few days, while they made presents to the relatives of Good-runner. Well, in the end Crow-eye became chief, but it was a sorry time for us all. As was the custom, my mother went to live with her people, or the Fat-roasting band. My mother's brother now took an interest in me. He gave me a gun. Guns were scarce in those days. My grandfather remembered when the first gun came to us and said that his father knew when the first horse came. I now spent much of my time with my uncle, though I still looked upon the Small-robes band as my band. He helped me to buy a place in the Pigeon Society and every spring and summer I danced with them and sometimes helped guard the camp at night when the great camp circle was formed.

It was during the summer following my father's death that I was taken on my first buffalo hunt. Sometimes boys were severely whipped by the police if found joining in running buffalo before they were old enough. But now my uncle took me with him. As guns were scarce, we kept them for war, and killed buffalo with arrows. When we rode at the herd, I took after a young cow. She was very fleet, but at last I drew alongside and sent an arrow into her. When she fell I stood by in awe. My relations praised me and my mother tanned the skin to make a robe for me. I was now a hunter and always joined in the killing unchallenged.

That autumn my mother ceased to mourn and married a man in the Lone-eaters band. After this I saw little of her, for they camped apart and I stayed with my uncle, but danced with my father's band, the Small-robes. About this time my uncle explained to me the ways of women and the duties of a man, so I began to look forward to having a woman of my own. I began to practice on the flageolet and to seek meetings with the girls of the camp on the path to the water hole; but I knew that though I had become a hunter, I had yet to go to war and to become a man. The opportunity soon came, for I was now about fourteen years old.

One day my uncle said, "Now it is time for you to go to war. When the moon is full, I shall lead a party to the Crow country. You can be the water boy." You know how it was with us, a boy might be taken to war to do errands. This is how he got his experience.

My uncle had a war bundle, or medicine, in which were a collar of coyote skin, a bird to tie in his hair, some tobacco, a pipe, paints, a whistle

and a rattle. Every night we gathered in his tepee to sing the songs of his bundle and to work out the plan for our raid. At last, we were off, eight of us. Though still a boy, I was permitted to take my gun, my bow, and a knife. As we were leaving the tepee my old grandmother asked me not to go; she took my hand and began to wail, but I pulled away. At the edge of the camp stood my uncle's father-in-law. He pled for all to return. Said he, "I have many horses, more than you can get from the Crow. Take what you want and stay at home. I am old and have not long to be with you." But we marched by in silence.

Pranks are usually played upon a boy on his first war excursion. The first night one of the warriors said, "Take this pail and run down that path for water, it is far." I set out briskly only to step into a deep pool of ill-smelling mud. About this I was teased, and all manner of jokes were made. Of course, the warriors knew the pool was there. They joked about my new paint, my new way of deceiving an enemy, my new perfume (love medicine), and so on. Finally one man in a very solemn manner conferred a new name upon me—Stinking-legs. From that time on, all of them called me by that name.

But by the next night we were in the open country and there was little hilarity. My uncle opened his bundle and performed the ritual for it, all of us singing in a low subdued tone. After this we traveled mostly by night and slept by day, though the warriors took turns scouting. On the fourth day, a scout reported the enemy.

"Now," said my uncle, "it is time to sing the 'tapping-the-stick'." So we all sat in a circle and my uncle began singing very softly, keeping time by tapping lightly on the stock of his gun with the end of his pipe-stick. He sang about a love affair and at the end named the woman. So it went around the circle. The last man, next to me, sang, and then named a young girl I was very fond of. Instinctively, I grasped my knife, but then, Oh shame! I was not yet a warrior, for here no one must resent. So I desisted, but I lay awake the rest of the day struggling with my anger. This was all very foolish, for the man was only teasing me; yet few men would venture to jest in such songs.

That night we stole out and found the Crow camp unguarded. So we took all the loose horses grazing outside and made off with them. Not even a dog barked. When at a safe distance my uncle told us to follow a warrior named Running-crane, that he and one man were going back to get scalps to pay for my father's death, that they would join us at the rendezvous later. My uncle was accompanied by the man who sang about my girl. On the third day my uncle overtook us, but he was alone. What became of his companion he knew not; he was never seen after they separated to steal into the Crow camp. That was what came of jesting with medicine songs. All holy things must be respected. But my uncle had brought a scalp, a shield, and a gun. So we were happy. When we got home there was feasting and scalp dancing for all. Finally, my old grandmother drew me out into full view, harangued the crowd upon my greatness as a warrior and said, "Now you must have been given a new name. What is it?" I hung my head for shame, "Oh!" she said, "my grandson is modest."

Then my uncle came forward and told the story of the mud hole and called me, "Stinking-legs." Then merriment broke loose and for a long time I was teased about it.

Two of the captured horses were allotted to me : one I gave to my grandfather. Not long after my uncle told me it was time to seek power. This meant that I must fast and sacrifice, seeking a vision. So I took my other Crow horse to old Medicine-bear, a shaman, offered him a pipe, and made my request. My instruction took many weeks. I was introduced to the sweat house and other ceremonies, learned how to make the pipe offering, to cry for power, and so forth. At last all was ready and old Medicine-bear left me alone on a high hill to fast, dance, and pray. Each evening and morning he came and, standing afar off, exhorted me to greater efforts. By the third day I was too exhausted to stand. That night I lay on my back looking up at the sky. Then I saw the Smoking-star.[1] And as I gazed it came nearer and nearer. Then I heard a voice, "My son, why do you cry here?" Then I saw a fine warrior sitting on the ground before me, smoking my pipe. At last he said, "I will give you power. You are to take my name. You must never change it. Always pray to me and I will help you."

The next morning when old Medicine-bear came and stood afar off I said, "Something has been given me." Then he prayed and took me home. In due time he heard my story, composed a song for me, gave me a small medicine bundle and announced my new name. I was now a man

---

1. Meaning: "the star who smoked my pipe."

of power. Many young men offered to go to war with me, so I soon began to lead out parties. Many coups I counted as the years passed, but all came by the power of the Smoking-star. Only once did this power seem to fail me on the war-path. I was alone and surrounded by the Cree. At last I called upon the Sun, offering to give him my little finger. Then I overcame my enemies. So at the next sun dance I chopped off this finger (the left) and offered it to the sun to fulfil my vow. But this belongs to the second period in my life, of which I shall speak later.

Shortly after I saw the Smoking-star, I took a woman. My uncle and my grandparents had often hinted of marriage. I was particularly fond of a girl in the Small-robe band, but could not court her openly because that was my band by right of my father, though I lived with the band of my mother, the Fat-roasters. It is not good for a man to marry in his own band where most of his relatives live, but he can freely marry a woman of his mother's band, if not too closely related to her. I could have joined my mother's band, as my uncle urged, and then married the girl, but that seemed to me like evading my duty to uphold the honor of my father and to take revenge for his untimely death. People would talk about it. So I courted a girl in my mother's band. As she was not closely related to me, there was no hindrance. Our courtship was secret, as is often the custom; when I led out my first war party she slyly passed me a pair of moccasins. I think no one knew of our attachment. You see my mother's people all looked upon me as one of their band, though they should not have done so, and so looked elsewhere for my future woman. Long afterward I learned that they had picked a woman for me from the Blood band, the widow of a young warrior, a good woman some ten years older than I, but it turned out otherwise.

The girl I courted was named Elk-woman. She and I were nearing twenty and it was time for her to marry, past time in fact. So her relatives arranged to give her to a man of the They-don't-laugh-band. The relatives of both parties had feasted and talked over the affair and were about ready to exchange the first presents, when Elk-woman's relatives first suggested the marriage to her. She asked for time to think it over. That evening when I met her as usual in a secret place, she told me the story and cried. Such a marriage was repugnant to her. I knew the man and had already come to dislike him. So that night we ran away. I took my horse, gun, and bow. We rode double. We went far up into the foothills of the mountains and made a secret camp.

Some two weeks later my uncle trailed us and we had a talk. He said I had done a very foolish thing; that all of my woman's relatives were angry and that the prospective husband vowed vengeance. However, as he had himself made the man a present of a horse and smoked a pipe with him, his anger was waning. He thought that since I had always adhered to my father's band I should go there to live. Anyway my father's people would then protect me. In due time presents could be made to my parents-in-law. You see when a man takes a woman, he is required to give many presents to her parents; this is called paying for her. So, I had stolen my woman because nothing had been paid. This would always stand against me in the minds of the people.

The next day we went back to my father's band. A poor old woman, an aunt of my father, one of my grandmothers, as we say, took us in as we had no tepee. No one seemed to take notice of us. When I hunted I took some of the meat and left it by the door of my father-in-law, as was the custom. Finally, my uncle's relatives got together and collected six horses, a few robes, a warrior's suit, and a great lot of dried meat. In solemn procession they paraded over to the camp of my parents-in-law. Then followed a feast and a reconciliation.

Not long after this I happened to meet my mother-in-law in a path. No one must see the face of his mother-in-law; if he does he must make her a present to cover her shame. This accident cost me my gun. It was a grievous loss as we were still poor. My woman had not so much as a travois-dog to bring wood.

At this point the narrator paused and began to fill his pipe. Presently he said, "The Smoking-star is still overhead. We have reached the fork of the first trail; the boy becomes a hunter, goes to war, has a vision, he joins the Pigeons, then marries and takes his place among the men of his band. So far he travels but one trail. Thenceforth it is different with us, some become warriors, some medicine men, some are chiefs. It is well that we rest here a little while, before I go on."

When the pipe was burned out the story began thus:—

Some time before I was married I bought into the Mosquito society when they sold out to the Pigeons. It was this way with us: There were nine societies for men, of different rank as follows; Mosquitoes, Braves, All-brave-dogs, Front-tails, Raven-bearers, Dogs, Kit-foxes, Catchers,

and Bulls. Lower than all was a boy's society, the Pigeons. To enter these societies you first bought into the Pigeons; that is, you gave presents to an older member who in return transferred his membership to you. Every four years each of the nine men's societies sold to the next lower; so one might finally, if he lived to be an old man, become a member of the Bulls. These societies were spoken of as the All-comrades. Each had its own songs, dances, regalia, and ritual. When the whole tribe came together for the summer hunt and the sun dance, these societies were called upon to guard and police the camp. Their parades and dances through the camp were very impressive. As all the members of a society were near the same age, these organizations are often called age-societies by the white people.

In time I passed through all of the societies and became a Bull. When in the Raven-bearers we gave a dance at a trading post where Fort Benton now stands and two strange white men watched us. One of them drew a picture of us and afterwards the older man asked questions of me through an interpreter and wrote something in a book. I heard that he came from across the great water as did the first white people, but I never saw him again.

When with my comrades in the Bulls we sold out to the Catchers, I became one of the old men to sit in council and advise the people. There are two leaders for each society. I was never a leader, because the leaders of one always sold to the leaders of the lower, and it so happened during my life that the same two men lived to reach the Bulls. So there was no chance for anyone else to lead. But we are now far ahead of my story, I must begin with my life as one of the young married men.

After I came back with my woman to live in my band, old Medicine-bear often sat in our tepee. (My woman soon tanned skins from my hunting and made a large fine tepee of our own.) He wished me to become a shaman like himself. You see I had experienced a real vision, few men who fasted received such power as came to me. I had the power to become a shaman, but I held to my vow to be a warrior. I was poor. So I led war parties against the Cree, Assiniboin, Snake, and Crow. Many horses and guns I took. Coups I counted and took three scalps from the Crow. But I meditated often upon the powers in the air, water, and earth. They are the great mysteries. Everything is done by them. About this time two things happened to me that turned my thoughts from war.

Our chief led a party against the Cree and invited me to go. The chief was jealous of me. As I told you, he was a bad man, but I could not refuse. Medicine-bear, the shaman, went with us to give us power. When we reached the Cree country I was ordered out as a scout. It was dark. As I went along I saw a tepee all by itself. I went up to it quietly and looked in. There was no one in the tepee except a man, his wife, and a little child. The little child could just walk and was amusing itself by dipping soup from the kettle with a small horn spoon. The man and his wife were busy talking and paid no attention to the child. Now the child looked up and saw me peeping through the hole, toddled over to the kettle, dipped up some soup in the spoon and held it to my lips. I drank and the child returned to the kettle for more. In this way the child fed me for many minutes. Then I went away. As I went along to my own party, I thought to myself, "I do not like to do this, but I must tell my party about this tepee. When they know of it, they will come and kill these people. This little child fed me even when I was spying upon them, and I do not like to have it killed. Well, perhaps I can save the child; but then it would be too bad for it to lose its parents. No, I do not see how I can save them, yet I cannot bear to have them killed." I sat down and thought it over. After a while, I went back to the tepee, went in, and sat down. While my host was preparing the pipe, the child began to feed me again with the spoon. After we had smoked, I talked to the man in the sign-language, told him all about it, how I had come as a scout to spy upon them, how I was about to bring up my war party, but that they had been saved by the little child. Then I directed the man to go at once, leaving everything behind him in the tepee.

The man was very thankful and offered to give me a medicine bundle and a suit of clothes; but I refused, because I knew that my party would suspect me. Then the man suggested that he might place the bundle near the door, behind the bedding, so that when the war party came up and dashed upon the tepee, I would be the first to capture the bundle. (All the important property of the tepee is always kept at the back, opposite the door, and, when a war party rushes in, the swiftest runs to this place.)

Then I reported to my chief, telling him that I had discovered a camp of the enemy but that I had not been up to it or seen anyone. He started out at once, all of us following. When we had surrounded the tepee, we gave a whoop and rushed upon it. I kept behind and while the others were busy counting coup upon the things in the back of the tepee, I seized the bundle by the door. The chief was angry, but said nothing. When we were again in camp old Medicine-bear began to unwrap his war medicine-pipe to make a thank offering for our success. Then the chief faced me and denounced me as a traitor, accused me of warning the enemy and secreting the medicine bundle. My anger rose, I drew my knife, but at that moment old Medicine-bear sprang between us, holding the holy pipe in both hands. This is the custom, no one can fight over a holy pipe. The shaman made us each take the pipe and vow to put away our anger and hold our silence. So it was.

Never have I forgotten that little child. Some great power was guarding it. Its medicine was strong. Many times have I prayed to that power and sometimes it helped me, but I do not yet know what power it is. Yet somehow I took little interest in war, the child's medicine did that to me. The next year I felt sad and gloomy. So I decided to go to war anyway. I led out a party of my own against the Crow. The fourth night I went out to scout. It was cloudy and rather dark. As I was stealing along a marshy place, a star rose out of the earth and stood before me. It was the Smoking-star. Something in me said, "Follow." Then the star led off slowly; gradually it took me to the back trail and then swiftly faded away, as it moved toward my woman's tepee at home. I sat down and prayed. In my mind the Smokingstar was telling me to go back.

When dawn came I returned to my party. I told my story. All agreed that we should go home for the signs were against us. When I got into our camp I saw many people standing about my woman's tepee and heard a doctor's drum. My son, my first born, was very ill. Three doctors had been called, one after the other. I gave them all my horses. As is their way, when they feared the sick one would die, they departed. At last, I went out to the top of a hill to cry to the Smoking-star. Surely, I thought, he would help me, but clouds overcast the sky and there was no answer to my appeal. That morning the boy died.

In the afternoon the body was wrapped in a robe and placed in a tree near our camp. As he died in the tepee, we could not use it again so we placed it at the foot of the tree. I cropped my hair and mourned many days. Now I was poor. All my horses went to the doctors. My woman's tepee was gone and once again we lived with our poor old grandmother in her little ragged tepee; but in a few days my woman's relatives gave her another tepee and after a time we again accumulated horses.

1073.

About this time Medicine-bear became a beaver bundle owner. My misfortunes turned my mind more and more to the mysteries of the powers around us and I began to learn the songs and the teachings of the beaver men. The ritual for the beaver bundle is long and difficult. There are more than three hundred songs to be learned before one can lead the ceremony of the beaver. In the bundle are the skins of beavers, otters, and many kinds of birds and water animals. With each of these there are songs, for each brought some power to the man who first saw it in a vision. My people did not plant corn, as did the Mud-houses (Mandan and Hidatsa), but the beaver men planted tobacco. At the planting and the gathering of the tobacco, the beaver bundle is opened and the ritual sung. The garden and the plants are sacred, for tobacco must be offered to all the powers of the earth, and of the water. A beaver man must keep count of the days, the moons, and the winters. For this he keeps a set of sticks like those sometimes found in a beaver's house. At all times he must be ready to tell the moon and the day; he must say when it is time to go on the spring hunt, to hold the sun dance, etc. Then he must watch the sun, moon, stars, winds, and clouds so that he may know what the weather will be. If he is holy and good, he will have visions and dreams of power and so become a shaman.

So after my son died I often sat with the beaver men. In time I learned many of the beaver songs and became chief assistant to Medicine-bear in the ceremonies. When I was an old man, Medicine-bear died; it was the year before I sold out of the Bull society (the year we saw the first steamboat). Then I became the leading beaver man, as I am still.

When I first began to study the beaver medicine, I spent hours on the hilltops and near the waters, meditating and watching the birds, animals, and the heavens. Yet such solemn thoughts did not occupy all my time as a young married man.

There was much sport in the winter camps. Many men played the wheel and arrow game and again the hand game. These were the favorite gambling games. The first was for two players, but the latter permitted team playing. Some men gambled away all their belongings and even their women. I never went so far. Once I remember two young men played the wheel game until one lost all his possessions except his moccasins and his breechcloth, finally losing these, to the great merriment of the whole camp.

My band had a great reputation for jokes. In this I was a leader. Once in the spring we fooled a man named Bow-string. This man had a favorite race horse which he guarded very carefully, picketing him outside his tepee. One day I dressed myself to look like a Crow, and while Bow-string was inside playing the hand game, untied his horse and led him off up the hills across the creek. Then a confederate gave the alarm. All ran out to see a Crow going off with the horse in broad day. Of course, everyone knew the trick, but Bow-string. Care had been taken to send all the other horses of the camp out to pasture with a herder. So Bow-string took a gun and set out with a pursuing party, afoot. Everybody in camp appeared to be greatly frightened, women screamed, and all the dogs began to bark. As the supposed Crow, I sprang upon the horse, waved a defiance and dashed over the hill.

Once out of sight I rode quickly around the hills and got back to camp after the pursuers had passed over the ridge. After a fruitless search for the trail, the party came back, Bow-string looking very sad. But there stood his horse tied as before! Then there was great uproar and jesting.

A favorite trick of mine was often played upon visiting strangers, especially upon dignified old men. I would invite the guest to my tepee to feast with a few of my friends. Then I would pretend to quarrel with my woman and we would fall to fighting. The others would try to separate us and so all begin to struggle, taking care to fall upon and thoroughly muss up the puzzled visitor.

Our people were fond of liquor, which could be had when we went to the trading posts in summer. At such times there was much fighting. We all wanted liquor because we believed that some mysterious power could be had in that way. Some men had visions while drunk, that made them shamans or doctors according to the powers that were given them. Sometimes I drank liquor too. Once when my woman was drunk also, we quarreled and I threatened to tomahawk her smallest child, but she snatched a burning stick from the fire and thrust the glowing end against my neck; you see the scar. After that I did not drink much. I was glad when the Great Father stopped the trading of liquor, it did us much harm. Once a year in summer all the bands of our tribe camped together.

A great circle of tepees was formed and the societies had charge of the camp. At this time the sun dance was held. It was very sacred and lasted

many days. No man was wise enough to know how all parts of it were conducted, so many medicine men were needed for the different rituals. Some men would vow to torture themselves at this time. I once gave a finger to the sun, but that is not the real sacrifice. Those who made the vow have holes cut in the skin of their breasts and shoulders, through which sticks are thrust and cords attached. The ends of these cords are fastened to the center pole in the sun-dance lodge, where these devotees dance and cry for power until they tear themselves free or fall in a swoon: I never made this sacrifice. I was afraid, for it is very holy. Yet many times have I given bits of my skin to Natos (the sun) as the scars upon my body show. These were not given in the sun dance, but when I was fasting alone in the hills.

A good and virtuous woman may often save the lives of her relatives by making a vow to take the tongues at the sun dance. My woman did this in the year known as "Gambler-died-winter" (about 1845, according to most tribal counts). Her brother was about to die. So she went outside, looked up at the sun, and said, "I will take the tongue at the sun dance." Her brother got well. If she had not been a pure and good woman, he would have died. In due time old Medicine-bear, the beaver bundle man, was given a horse and called in to prepare her for the ordeal. During the spring a hundred buffalo tongues were sliced and dried. Only true women are permitted to slice them. If a woman cuts her finger or cuts a hole in her slice, she is turned out because she has not been true to her husband. At the proper time in the sun dance, as the sun is setting, the women who have vowed to take the tongues go forward and in turn, take up a piece of tongue and holding it up to the sun, declare their purity. It is the duty of any man, who knows the claim to be false to come forward with a challenge. My woman was not challenged. Everyone knew her to be pure and good.

Once she was the holy woman to give the sun dance. It was in the deep snow winter (about 1851) that she became ill. Many people were starving, for the buffalo had drifted far before the snowstorms. Then my woman addressed the sun, saying that she would give the sun dance, next year. Soon the people found buffalo and she got well.

A woman cannot give the sun dance alone, her man must also be good and brave. Both must fast four days and sit in the holy tepee.

The holy natoas bundle must be opened and the woman wear its sacred headdress, with the prairie turnip and carry the digging-stick used by the Woman-who-married-a-star. That winter we were camped on the Missouri. The following summer we went to Yellow River to give the sun dance.

Now, it is our way, that the woman who vows to give the sun dance must buy a natoas bundle. The power and right to the ritual thus come to her. For this, many horses, robes, and dried meat must be given. When we came to bring our bundle all the people of our band and our relatives in other bands were called upon to help us by gifts. After the sun dance we kept the natoas bundle in our tepee and cared for it as the ritual required. My woman was now a medicine woman. She did not sell her bundle. In the Blood-fought-among-themselves winter she died (about 1858). I put the bundle in her robe, set up her tepee on a high hill and left her there. That is our custom.

She was a good and true woman. After that I went to live with my son, as you now see. I never took another woman because the Smoking-star appeared to me in a dream and forbade it. In the course of time everyone came to look upon me as a shaman. No one will now walk before me as I sit in a tepee. In my presence all are dignified and orderly and avoid frivolous talk. Four times in my life the Smoking-Star has stood before me. All visions are sacred, as are some dreams, but when a vision appears the fourth time, it is very holy. Even a shaman may not speak of it freely. Many times have I gone to lonely places and cried out to the powers of the air, the earth, and the waters to help me understand their ways. Sometimes they have answered me, but all the truly great mysteries are beyond understanding.

In the year of the Camp-at-bad-waters-winter the Bull society sold out as I have said. That was the end of that society; there were but three of us left when we sold to the Catchers and those to whom we sold soon died. The ways of the white man were coming among us and many things were passing away. I was now an old man, fit only for sitting in council. I could no longer run buffalo, no longer go to war. So we have come to the last fork in the trail. I have smoked many pipes. I have sat in many councils, I have made many speeches to restrain our young men from rash and unjust actions. We are near the end. The Smoking-star will soon pass down in the west. Soon it will lead me to the sand hills where my spirit will wander about among the ghosts of buffalo, horses, and men. Your way is not our way, but you have loved us. Perhaps your spirit also may return to wander with us among the sand hills of our fathers. I pray that it may be so. Now, it is finished.

Thoughtfully I left that fireside to find my blankets. As I passed out through the night, I saw the "Smoking-star" sinking in the west. It shone to me with a new light. The next winter my old friend passed into the beyond. His body was laid on a tree scaffold near the favorite haunts of his band on Two Medicine River.

Clark Wissler

LITTLE-WOLF JOINS THE MEDICINE LODGE

I
IN THE LODGE OF THE MASTER

MATCIKINEU, Terrible-eagle, sat dozing in the dusk in his round, rush-mat wigwam. The fire smouldered, but random drafts, slipping in through the swinging mat that covered the door, encouraged little dancing flames to spring up, and these illumined the far interior of the lodge, so that it was possible to observe its furnishings down to the mustiest cranny.

Around the inner circumference of the wigwam, ran a broad rustic bench, supported by forked sticks and thickly strewn balsam boughs on which lay bearskin robes. The inner wall of the home was hung with woven reed mats, bearing designs in color, of angular figures and conventional floral motifs. Over Terrible-eagle's head, on smoke en-crusted poles, swung several mat-covered, oval bundles, festooned with age-blackened gourd rattles, war clubs, and utensils and weapons of unusual portent. These were his sacred war and hunting bundles, pack-ets of charms whose use and accompanying formulae he had obtained personally from the Gods, while fasting, or purchased at a great price from others more fortunate than he. For Terrible-eagle was a renowned war leader, a hunter, and the greatest of all Mate Mitawuk, Masters of the Grand Medicine Society, a secret fraternal and medical organization, to which, in one form or another, nearly every Indian of influence in all the Great Lakes and Central Western region belonged.

The door covering was quietly thrust aside and Anam, a Wolf-like dog, trotted in to curl up by the fire, while after him, first drop-ping a load of faggots from her shoulders, stumbled Wabanomitamu,

Dawn-woman, wife of Terrible-eagle, who crouched down grumbling to enter the lodge, and turned on her time-gnarled knees to drag the kindlings in after her.

Roused by the noise, Terrible-eagle stretched and yawned, then reached over his head and took down a calabash-shell rattle, which he began to shake gently, while Dawn-woman shoved aside the birch-bark boxes that cluttered the floor, stirred up the fire in the round, shallow pit where it was glowing, and set among the hot embers a large, round, deep, pointed-bottomed kettle of brown earthen-ware, the base of which she screwed into the ashes by a quick, circular twist of the rim. Into this kettle she poured some water from a birch-bark pail; and, when it began to simmer, added a quantity of wild rice, smoked meat, and dried berries, which she stirred with an elaborate wooden-spoon paddle. The random swish of Terrible-eagle's rattle now began to articulate itself in the form of a tune, the motif of which might have been borrowed from the night babblings and murmurings of a woodland brook. It rose like the prattle of water racing down stony riffles; it fell to the purring mono-tone of a little fall burbling into a deep pool.

Then, suddenly, Terrible-eagle raised his voice in song—a song without meaning to the uninitiated—yet a song potent with the powers of Manitous, and ancient as the pine forests.

"Ni manituk, hawatukuk, ke'neaminum."

"You, my gods, I am singing to you!"

"Look you, old fellow," cried Dawn-woman, squatting beside her cooking, "why do you sing that sacred song? There is no need to re-hearse the chants of the Manitous when ice binds the rivers, and snow blankets the land! When new life dawns with the grass blades in the spring, then we will need to refresh our memories; not now, while the gods sleep like bears."

"Silence, old partner! You do not know everything! Even now there comes one seeking the knowledge of the path our brethren and fellows have trod before us. Listen!"

The lodge was hushed with the heavy silence of the Wisconsin forest in midwinter. Then came the crunch and squeak of approaching snow-shoes slipping over the crusted drifts.

"N'hau, Dawn-woman! Prepare the guest place, spread robes behind the fire, dish out a bowl of soup! Some one of our people desires to enter!"

The noise ceased before the doorway, and Terrible-eagle, now hunched before the fire, paused before dropping a hot coal on the tobacco in his red stone pipe, to bid the guest to enter. "Yoh!" came the hearty response, and a tall, dark warrior, bareheaded save for a fillet of otter fur around his brows, ducked under the doorway and silently passed round the fire, on the left, to the guest place, where he seated himself, cross-legged, on a pile of robes. He was clad in a plain shirt of blue-dyed deerskin, deeply fringed on the seams, in flapping, leather leggings, high soft-soled moccasins, and a leather apron handsomely embroidered with colored porcupine quills wrought in delicate, flowered figures. He bore no weapon, and on his swarthy cheeks two round spots of red paint were seen in the firelight.

After the newcomer had eaten a bowl of steaming stew with the aid of a huge, wooden ladle, he lay back among the robes, puffing comfortably on a long-stemmed pipe with bowl of red stone, filled and lighted for him by the old man. As the cheerful odor of tobacco and kinnikinick permeated the lodge, the stranger began to speak. He informed the old people that his name was Muhwase, Little-wolf, of the Wave clan of the Menomini, that he had come all the way from Mate Suamako, the Great Sand Bar village on the Green Bay of Lake Michigan; that the young men had opened their war bundles, and danced preparatory to going to war against the Sauk, but that the Sauk had heard the news and fled southward. He ended with all the gossip and tittle-tattle of his band.

It was not until Dawn-woman slept, and the stars were visible in the winter sky through the smoke hole of the lodge, that Little-wolf went out abruptly, and returned bearing a huge bundle which he dumped on the floor at the feet of Terrible-eagle, and silently took his place on the lounge once more.

With trembling hands the old man undid the leathern thongs and unwrapped the bearskin with which the bundle was enclosed, and spread before him an array of articles that brought an avaricious sparkle to his red-rimmed eyes.

"Nima, nekan! Well done, my colleague!" he exclaimed. "These are valuable gifts, and in the proper number. Four hatchets, four spears, and four knives of the sacred yellow rock (native copper), four belts of white wampum, and four garments of tanned deerskin, embroidered with quillwork, with much tobacco. Surely this gift has a meaning?"

"Grandfather! You to whom nothing is hard," replied the visitor. "It is true that I am nobody. I am poor—the enemy scarcely know my name. Yet I am desirous of eating the food of the Medicine Lodge, as all the brethren have done who have passed this way before me!"

"N'hau, my grandson! I shall call together the three other Push-wawuk, or masters, for their consent. What you have asked for, may seem as nothing to you—yet it is Life. These songs may appear to partake of the ways of children—yet they are powerful. I understand you well; you desire to imitate the ways of our own ancient Grand Master, Ma'nabus, who was slain and brought to life that we might gain life unending! Good! You have done well. In the morning I shall send invitation-sticks and tobacco to summon the leaders here, that your instruction may begin at once!"

II
THE INSTRUCTION

It was an hour after sunset. In the rear of the lodge sat Terrible-eagle and three other old men, with Little-wolf at their left. Before them lay the pile of valuable gifts, and, on the white-tanned skin of an unborn fawn, stood the sacred towaka or deep drum, hollowed by infinite labor from a short section of a basswood log, holding two fingers' depth of water to make its voice resonant, and covered with a dampened membrane of tanned, buck hide. Across its head was balanced a crooked drumstick, its striking end carved to represent a loon's beak. Before the drum, was placed a wooden bowl in the shape of a miniature, log canoe heaped with tobacco, and four gourd rattles with wooden handles which shone from age and usage. A youth tended the fire and kept the air redolent with incense of burning sweet grass and cedar. Dawn-woman and Anam, the dog, guarded the door.

Extending his hands over the sacred articles before them, Terrible-eagle began a prayer of invocation, calling on the mythical hero and founder of the Medicine Lodge, Ma'nabus, on the Great Spirit, the Sun, and the Thunderbirds; on the good-god Powers or Manitous of air and earth, and also upon the Evil Powers who dwell in and under the earth and water and hidden in the dismal places of the world, to appear in spirit and accept the tobacco offered them and to dedicate the fees presented to the instructors.

When the prayer was ended, all those gathered in the wigwam ejaculated "Hau," and three of the elders smoked and listened while Terrible-eagle began the instruction by relating the history of the origin of the Medicine Lodge. Taking the drumstick in his hand, Terrible-eagle gave four distinct strokes on the drum, and recited in a rhythmic and solemn tone, hushing his voice to a whisper when it became necessary to mention a great Power by name.

He told how Mate Hawatuk, the Great Spirit, sat alone in the heavenly void above the ever extending sea, and willed that an island (the world) should appear there; how he further willed that there should spring up upon this island, an old woman who was known as "Our Grandmother, The Earth." He recited how the Earth Grandmother conceived, supernaturally, and gave birth to a daughter. How the Four winds, desiring to be born as men, entered the daughter's body and lay as twins in her womb, and how, when the hour of their birth came, so great was their power, they burst their mother, making women forever after liable to death in travail.

"Then," related Terrible-eagle, "our Earth Grandmother gathered up the shattered pieces of her daughter, and placed them under an inverted, wooden bowl, and prayed, and on the fourth day, through the pity of the Great Spirit, the fragments were changed into a little rabbit, who was named Mate Wabus, or the Great Hare, since corrupted into 'Ma'nabus,' who was to prepare the world for human habitation.

"The rabbit grew, in human form, to man's estate, when he was given, as a companion and younger brother, a little wolf, but the Powers Below, being jealous, slew the wolf brother. Then, Ma'nabus in his wrath attacked the Powers below, and, as he was the child of the Great Spirit, they could not resist him. In fear the Evil Powers restored his younger brother to life, but, since he had been dead four days, the flesh dropped from his bones and he stank, and Ma'nabus, in sorrow, refused to receive him, and sent him to rule the dead in the After World, at the end of the Milky Way in the Western Heavens. Hence, human beings may not come back to life on the fourth day.

"At their wits' end to appease Ma'nabus, the Evil Ones called on the Powers Above who are of good portent. They erected a Medicine Lodge

Cree Indian

on the high hilltops, oblong, rectangular, facing east and west. The Power of the Winds roofed it with blue sky and white clouds. The pole framework was bound with living, hissing serpents instead of basswood strings, the food for feasting was seasoned with a pinch of the blue sky itself. Then the Powers entered. The gods of Evil took the north side where darkness and cold abide; the Good Powers Above sat on the south. Then they all stripped off the animal natures with which they were disguised, and hung them on the wall of the Lodge, and all appeared in their true forms, as aged persons.

"In council, guided by the admonitions of the Great Spirit, they decided to give to Ma'nabus the ritual of the Lodge, with its secret—long life and immortality for mankind—as a bribe to cease his molestation. But Ma'nabus refused to receive their message, until Otter volunteered to fetch him. Then Ma'nabus came, and was duly instructed and raised, by being slain and brought to life again, thus showing the great potency of the Powers who owned the Lodge.

"This very ceremony, just as it was given Ma'nabus, and later transferred to us, his uncles and aunts, with its rites, formulas, and medicines, is the same," concluded Terrible-eagle, "as we perform to-day, as all the brethren and fellows have done who have passed this way before us, since the Menomini came out of the ground, in the past." As he ended the old man struck the drum four times, crying, "My colleagues, my colleagues, my colleagues, my colleagues!"

When Terrible-eagle had concluded his part, there was a recess for refreshment and relaxation, which lasted until each had smoked, then another old pushwao or master took up the work. He it was who related to the candidate the identity of the Powers Above and Below who had given the Medicine Lodge to mankind, through Ma'nabus. There were, he said, four groups of Evil Powers, who sat on the north side of the Lodge. First were the Otter, Mink, Marten, and Weasel; second the Bear, Panther, Wolf, and Horned Owl; third the Banded Rattlesnake, the little Prairie Rattlesnake, the Pine Snake, and the Hog-nosed Snake. The fourth group was composed of lesser birds and beasts. The Upper World which had not offended Ma'nabus, was not so well represented, and was composed of various predatory birds, such as the Red-shouldered Hawk and the Sparrow-hawks. These sat on the south side, and, in ancient days, human Lodge members had been seated according to the nature of their medicine bags.

The skins of any of these animals might be used as containers or sacks for the secret nostrums of the craft, but the Dog and Fox, which were formerly associated with the Wolf, had, by their cunning and their custom of eating filth and carrion, become too closely associated with witchcraft, and were now tabu.

The old master then told the candidates that each of these animals had donated some special power to aid mankind. Thus the Weasel gave cunning and ferocity in war and the chase, the Snapping-turtle, probably one of the vague fourth group of Evil Powers, had given his heart, which beats long after it is torn from his bosom, to grant long life. Each animal had four songs sung in his honor during the session of the Lodge, said the elder, and the third instructor would teach these to the candidate.

The old master informed his pupil that in his opinion the Medicine Lodge and its rites were found far to the east, in the country by the Great Sea Where the Dawn Rises, for he had once met a party of warriors, from the far off Nottoway or Iroquois, who spoke of a society and its ritual, given them by the animals, which had for its object long life and immortality for men.

Dawn-woman now fetched steaming rice and fat venison, marrow-bones and dried berries, and the little party feasted. The hour was very late, yet none thought of sleep. After the feast, the third elder did his part.

He selected a calabash rattle, and, sometimes rattling, sometimes drumming an accompaniment, taught the songs of the Lodge to Little Wolf. There were songs of opening and songs of closing, as well as the animal songs, each repeated four times, the sacred number, and each in groups of four. Each was made obscure and unintelligible to eavesdroppers by the addition of nonsense syllables. Some, indeed, were so ancient, and so clouded by vocables, that nothing but their general meaning was remembered even by the brethren. These passed for songs in a secret, magic language. Some chants were in other languages, particularly Ojibway, and all ended with the mystic phrase "we-ho-ho-ho-ho," which meant "so mote it be." The songs had titles, but these names too, were magic, and often gave no inkling of the meaning or wording of the song, and most of them avoided naming the animals or gods to which they referred, except by circumlocution, or by merely mentioning some prominent characteristic or attribute of the creature.

There were songs for the "shooting of the medicine"—an act which was so secret and mysterious that the candidate was as yet kept in the dark as to its meaning—and others for dancing, for thanksgiving and for dedication.

When the third elder had ended his synopsis of the songs, which the candidate had later to purchase and learn at leisure, the fourth and last past master took him in hand. His part, he said, was short, yet important. He showed the candidate certain articles which would be ceremonially given to the candidate at the proper time and place. Among these articles was the tanned skin of an otter, the nostrils of which were stuffed with tufts of red-dyed hawk-down, the under surfaces of the four feet and tail being adorned with fringed rectangles of blue-dyed doe leather, embroidered with conventional flower designs in colored porcupine hair and quills. This was to be the medicine bag of the new member. Through an opening, a slit in the chest of the otter, one could thrust a hand, and find in the little pouch made by the skin of the left forefoot of the animal, a small sea shell, called the konapamik, or medicine arrow, by which the essence of all the sacred objects contained in the bag was ceremonially "shot" or transferred to the bodies of the Lodge brethren during the performance of the ritual.

Three other medicines the otter skin contained. There were sacred, blue face-paint, the color of the sky; a mysterious brown powder holding a seed, wrapped in a packet with a fresh water clamshell; and another mixture of pounded roots called "Reviver," or Apisetchikun.

The clamshell was a sacred, ancient cup, in which the accompanying powder and seed were placed with a little water, and given to all candidates to drink. The mystic seed was supposed to be the badge of the Medicine Lodge, and was to remain in the candidate's breast, forever, even until he had followed the Pathway of the Dead along the Milky Way. The "Reviver" was a powerful drug for use at all times when life ebbed low, through sickness or magic.

"These then," said the last instructor, "are the ways and sacred things of Ma'nabus, given us Indians to have and use, as long as the world shall stand!"

So saying, he in turn retired, and the party rolled in their blankets to sleep before the sun could look in through the smoke hole of the wigwam.

"Os-Ko-Bos"
(Chippewa)
No. 2.

Chippewa Indians, Detroit Lakes, Minn. L-616

III
THE INITIATION

It was the season when buds burst, and the young owls, hatched while the snow was yet on the ground, were already taking their prey. The discordant croaking of the frogs came as a roar from the marshlands. The arbutus was blooming.

Perched on the top of a warm, sunny knoll, was an oblong, dome-roofed structure of poles, covered with bark and rush mats. It was oriented east and west, and its length, a full hundred feet, contrasted oddly with its breadth of twenty.

It was the evening of the fourth day of the Mitawiwin, or Medicine ceremony. The preceding three days and nights had been spent by the four masters, led by Terrible-eagle, in preparing Little-wolf within a room, formed by curtaining off one end of the lodge proper; in giving him his ceremonial sweat bath of purification; and in hanging the initiation fees, four sets of valuable goods—clothing, robes, weapons, copper utensils—on the ridgepole at the eastern end of the lodge; and in dedicating them.

As the sun set, the four old men and the candidate entered the lodge, followed by the men and women of the tribe who were already members of the society. Going in at the eastern door, the procession filed along the north side, and passing once regularly around, the people seated themselves on the right of the door, with the candidate on the west side of them, next to Terrible-eagle.

The night having largely passed in quiescence and instruction, towards dawn an officer of the lodge approached Little-wolf, and stood before him, facing the east. Thrusting his hand into his medicine bag he drew forth his sacred clamshell cup and the powder containing the seed, which he compounded into a drink, while he sang a song called "What Otter Keeps."

"I am preparing the thing that was hung [the little seed], And that which was hung shall fall!"

When he had finished, and Little-wolf had swallowed the draft, this officer retired, and another came forward and took his place, singing. As he ended, he stooped over, coughed and retched violently until he cast forth a sea shell, which he held in the palm of his hand, and, chanting, displayed to the east, west, south, and north, after which he caused Little-wolf to swallow it, that it might remain in his body forever: the symbol of immortality, and the badge of a lodge member. When this had been accomplished the assistant gave place to a third, who sang his four songs and painted the candidate's face with the sacred, blue paint. Then a fourth and last assistant came before the candidate and the masters, bearing an otter-skin, medicine bag, which he laid at Little-wolf's feet, while he sang four songs concerning Otter, the most famous of which was entitled Yom Mitawakeu, or "This Medicine Land," but which held no reference to otters whatever!

Now the old men conducted the candidate, four times regularly around the lodge, while they related to him somewhat of the story of the ancient Master Ma'nabus, whom he now represented. On the last circuit

Chach-scheb-nee-nick-ah (Young
Winneba

Terrible-eagle led him to a seat near the western end of the lodge, and there placed him, facing the east; remaining with the candidate standing behind, and holding his shoulders.

The men and women seated around the walls of the lodge sat tense. The silence was unbroken save for woodland sounds, for the great, dramatic moment had arrived.

The four assistant masters, who had just performed before Little-wolf, now assembled in the east, facing him, and the first, taking his medicine bag in his two hands, and holding it breast high before his body, sang, to the rapid beat of the drum, a song entitled "Shooting the New Member." At its end he gave the usual sacred cry "oh we ho ho ho ho!" blew on the head of the otter skin, and rushed forward as though to attack the candidate.

In front of the neophyte impersonator of the ancient hero the attacker paused, and jerked the head of his otter upward, crying savagely, "Ya ha ha ha ha!" The magical essence of the bag supposedly striking the candidate, he staggered slightly, but was steadied by a companion, only to meet the feigned attacks of the second and third assistants, at each of which he reeled once more.

But the charge of the fourth fellow was so violent that the candidate fell flat on the ground. Stooping, the last man laid the medicine bag across the back of the apparently unconscious brother, to be his, there-after. At a sign from Terrible-eagle, the four assistants approached the prostrate candidate, and raising him to his feet, shook him gently to remove their shots and restore him to life. And now all was rejoicing. Steaming earthen kettles were carried in, filled with delicious stews and soups of bear and turtle flesh, partridges, and young ducks. Laughing, jesting, and good-natured banter filled the lodge until the last wooden bowl was scraped clean, when the utensils and scraps were carried out, and the drummer struck up a lively dancing tune. After the men and women had had each four sets of songs, a general dance took place, wherein the members circled the lodge, the new brother among them, shooting each other promiscuously with jollity, vying with each other to rise and point their bags or fall prone on the earth. All the time a loud and lively chant was sung :

I

"I pass through them! I pass through them! I pass through even the chief!"

II

"Ye Gods take part, invisible though ye be beneath us!"

When all was over, and Keso, the Sun, was almost noon high, the four assistants took down the invitation fees from the ridgepole, and distributed them to the four old Masters and the others who had taken prominent part in the ceremonial, and all the Indians filed out of the western door, singing:

"You, my brethren, I pass my hand over you. I thank you."

Muhwase, Little-wolf, watched the last of his companions strike their camps; saw the coverings stripped from the lodge structure, saw the last party vanish in the brush.

He was a Mitao! A member of a great fraternal organization, who might travel westward to the foothills of the Rockies, north to the Barren Lands, south to the countries of the Iowa and Oto, east to the land of the Iroquois, and find brethren who had traveled the same road, or at least one fundamentally similar. He had shown his fortitude and fidelity, those two great, cardinal virtues of the Medicine Lodge, and he had come through the sacred mysteries alive and in possession of the secret rites that had been handed down since the days when the Menomini first came out of the ground.

Alanson Skinner

Hanging-flower, the Iroquois

I

She was born in a bark house. Her mother, Rising-sun, was surprised as she looked at the little face, for she felt that once before, long ago, she had seen that face, and presently the assurance came to her that the child was the image of her great-grandmother, Rising-sun's mother's mother, whom she had often seen when she herself was a little girl. Hanging-flower had been a great medicine woman in her day, and the fame of her art had spread far and wide; on one occasion, it was claimed, she had even cured a woman of insanity. Rising-sun could not hesitate long: she wished to name the baby Hanging-flower.

Soon after this, when Rising-sun had regained her health and vigor, she called on Clear-as-a-brook, the Keeper of names of the Bear clan, to which Rising-sun belonged. From her the mother learned that Hanging-flower, a remote relative of Rising-sun, of whom she remembered having heard, had recently died and that her name had been "put away in a box." The mother knew now that nothing stood in the way of the realization of her desire: Hanging-flower was to be the name of her little girl.

When the fall came, Rising-sun began to get ready for the great Green Corn Festival, and on the second day of the festivities she carried little Hanging-flower to the Long House where her name was ceremonially bestowed upon her, in the presence of all the people.

II

The first summers of Hanging-flower's life passed uneventfully. Rising-sun was a kind mother; for hours she talked to little Hanging-flower
in soft, soothing tones, and at night she sang her to sleep with her dole-
ful, monotonous lullabies. When harvesting time came and Rising-sun
was busy in the cornfields with the other women, Hanging-flower was
wrapped and tied securely to her carrying-board, which was then hung
on a branch of an elm tree; there, gently swayed by the wind, Hanging-flower slept, while her mother was hard at work.

III

The summers passed, and Hanging-flower was a baby no longer. Her mother taught her the art of cooking; she also began to help when the corn was pounded in large, wooden mortars. Soon she learned how to embroider. And as her fingers grew nimble and her eyes fond of the colored beads and wampum shells, she began to feel that the world of buds and flowers and leaves was her own, hers and her mother's and of the other women;—the men knew nothing of such things.

Once, when Rising-sun's brother was staying for a visit, Hanging-flower overtook him at work on a small False Face; for a long time she watched him unobserved, and when he was gone, she practiced carving on bits of wood and bark until she felt that she was as good at it as any man. But of this she never spoke nor did she show her work to any one, as she had been taught that carving was not woman's work.

IV

The summers passed and Hanging-flower became a maiden. Her eyes were large, black and deep, and her hair which she wore in two large braids, fell heavily from her shoulders. As she passed along the road, some boys looked intently at her while others turned their eyes away and hurried their steps. But, one and all, she passed them by. Hanging-flower had become a great dancer, and many a flattering comment was heard among the older men and women as they watched her dance with the others at the Strawberry and Raspberry Festivals.

V

At the next berrying season Hanging-flower joined a group of young men and girls and together they went off to the woods. Old Ringing-voice, the great story-teller, was with them. Every night, when the day's work was done and the boys and girls returned to camp with their baskets heaped full of red, juicy berries, they would all sit around the fire, while Quick-of-hand and She-works-in-the-house, who were reputed for their skill in cooking, prepared a delicious soup of corn meal,

after which, berries in great quantities were eaten. Then Ringing-voice would light his pipe and leaning his back against a tree stump, the legs drawn up so that the knees almost touched his chin, he would begin to talk, in slow and measured phrases. It is here that Hanging-flower first learned of the language of the animals and of the great warrior who had been so kind to the beasts and birds of the woods and the fields, and who was brought to life by their efforts after he had succumbed to the arrows of the Sioux. She learned of the great medicine, ga'no-da, which the animals made of parts of their own bodies and gave to the warrior to be used as a cure for all sickness. She was thrilled as she listened to the story of Pale-face, the pure youth, who started out alone and, wandering through the woods, met the pygmies and learned from them the Pygmy or Dark Dance, which, her mother had told her, she would herself one day perform. And for many evenings in succession, the boys and girls were spellbound as Ringing-voice recounted the great story of the foundation of the League, of Deganawida and Hayenhwahtha, the great chiefs, who organized the League and prescribed the Law and established the Great Peace.

One night, as they were sitting around the fire, and Ringing-voice was absorbed in his tale, Hanging-flower suddenly became aware that some one was looking at her. She turned her head and saw Straight-as-an-arrow, the tall, slim youth, who was staring at her with large wondering eyes. She looked away, and not once during the long evening did she turn her head again.

Evening after evening, while listening to the stories, Hanging-flower felt his gaze fixed upon her. She never turned, she was afraid even to move, but she knew that his eyes were fixed upon her.

One night, when the moon was not shining and all was quiet in the camp, he came upon her like the wind. Seized with terror, Hanging-flower wanted to scream. Her lips parted, but no sound came; her heart was beating fast and she lay there in the wet grass, hot and trembling.

When next spring came a baby was born to Hanging-flower. It made no sound when it came, for it was dead. On the evening of that day, two forms, wrapped in blankets, slipped out of the bark house; one was carrying a small bundle in her arms. Quietly as shadows they glided along the road, until they reached the cemetery of the Bear clan. And there the

J. Grasset S.t Sauveur inv. direx

J. Laroque Sculp.

Iroquois

two women buried the little, nameless thing that had come unasked for and unwelcome. No one had seen them, no one knew; and after a while, Hanging-flower herself forgot what had happened.

VI

Some time later Rising-sun paid a visit to her sister's village. It so happened that the Bean Feast was being held at that time. Rising-sun went to the Long House with her sister and her people. There she saw Fleet-of-foot, the great runner, and so charmed was she with his form, graceful as that of a deer, that she could not take her eyes off him. After the feast, Rising-sun spoke to Fleet-of-foot's mother. She asked Corn-planter to visit her at the home village.

VII

In a little while, Corn-planter came to visit Rising-sun. With her hostess she went to the fields where the corn was ripe and the women were busy harvesting it. She saw the long rows of bent backs, and the green and yellow cobs which would show for an instant over the left shoulders of the women, presently to disappear into the large baskets on their backs.

"That young girl in the third row," exclaimed Corn-planter, "seems to do work for two. Look how her hands fly through the corn!"

"It is Hanging-flower," answered Rising-sun, "my daughter. And a good wife she would make for Fleet-of-foot, the runner."

"Let her cook a basket of corn bread," said Corn-planter, "Fleet-of-foot will be ready."

VIII

That night Rising-sun told Hanging-flower that the time had come for her to be married, and that Fleet-of-foot, the great runner, was ready to accept her basket of corn bread. Saying not a word, Hanging-flower got busy with the corn meal and before morning the basket of bread was ready. Hanging-flower started on her way early, and by noon she had reached Corn-planter's village. The boys were running races when she arrived. With wide open eyes she stood, as Fleet-of-foot rushed by her, as if carried by the wind. Hanging-flower shut her eyes... and it seemed to her that she heard the rustling of the pines; she felt herself lying in the wet grass, hot and trembling; and through the mist she saw two shapes wrapped in blankets, bending over a nameless thing which they buried in the ground....

When the races were over Hanging-flower saw Fleet-of-foot resting on a stump of wood in front of his mother's house. Then she stepped forward and placed the basket of corn bread before him on the ground. Fleet-of-foot rose and said nothing. He only looked at Hanging-flower with a sharp, piercing look and, taking the basket, entered the house. In a while Corn-planter appeared in the doorway. She invited Hanging-flower to step inside, and Hanging-flower had her meal with Corn-planter and her people. The sun was still high when she started on her way back and before nightfall she reached her village.

When Hanging-flower fell asleep that night she saw some deer running among the trees. One of the deer was larger and fleeter than the others. Hanging-flower was trying to catch it. Again and again she felt herself flying through the air, in pursuit, but just as she was about to seize it, it eluded her.

In the morning of the following day Fleet-of-foot arrived before the house where Hanging-flower lived with her people. As she saw him enter, she rose to her feet. In his hand he held a necklace of blue and white wampum beads. Presently he took them in both hands and placed them about her neck. Then Hanging-flower knew that she had a husband.

The Long House in which Hanging-flower had lived with her mother and several other families had been crowded for some time, and Fleet-of-foot decided that they had to start a new home for themselves. Many men and women, most of them relatives of Hanging-flower, helped the young couple to build a small bark house, and before many moons had passed the house was ready and Hanging-flower and Fleet-of-foot began to live there.

AHYOUWAIGHS

CHIEF OF THE SIX NATIONS.

PUBLISHED BY F. W. GREENOUGH, PHILAD.ª

Drawn Printed & Coloured at I.T. Bowen's Lithographic Establishment Nº 94 Walnut St.

Entered according to act of Congress in the Year 1838 by F. Wisenough, in the Clerks Office of the District Court of the Eastern District of Penn.ª

As the summers passed, other couples came to live in the house, and extensions were built to it, to accommodate the ever-growing numbers. This continued for some time, until the house became a Long House, like the others.

IX

When the next berrying season came, a son was born to Hanging-flower; and having consulted Spring-blossoms, her mother's mother, Hanging-flower gave him the name Glad-tidings. As Hanging-flower was lying on her bed and her blood was hot in her, she heard the sound of rattles outside and she saw her brother take his turtle rattle and join the False Faces, who were passing through the village. Hanging-flower knew that Glad-tidings was one day to become a chief, and that night she carved a little False Face and hid it in her bag, for she had heard the rattles and she knew that some day her son was to be a leader of the False Faces. Hanging-flower was very beautiful, as she lay there on her bed. Her large black eyes were even larger and deeper than usual; she had looked into the future.

X

Many summers passed and Glad-tidings had become a strong and handsome youth. He was very young, but the older men thought him wise and cool-headed. The women were wild over him, but he had no eyes for them. He would rather sit with the older men, always inquiring about ancient things and eager to learn the laws and traditions of his people.

One day, while Hanging-flower was pounding corn back of her house, a piercing sound was heard on the road, gwa-a! gwa-a! gwa-a! Hanging-flower shuddered, for she knew that a chief was dead. Soon the news came that Power-of-thunder, her brother, had been killed by a stray arrow during an encounter with the Sioux.

Spring-blossoms and Rising-sun were dead and Hanging-flower was the matron of her family now. When she heard the mournful news, she began to think of Glad-tidings. He was young, but wise and strong, and there was no other man in the family who might be made chief in his stead.

In a few days a Council of the family was called by Hanging-flower. There were some men at the Council, but mostly women, and although some other Bear people were there, most of those present belonged to Hanging-flower's family. When they were all assembled, Hanging-flower began to speak and as she spoke, all were silent. She spoke of Glad-tidings' youth, but recalled the many indications of wisdom and character which he had given, and before closing, she nominated her son to be chief in place of Power-of-thunder, her brother.

For many days after this, Hanging-flower was busy calling on the other chiefs of her tribe. First she called on those who belonged to the brother clans and then on those who were of the cousin clans, and when her nominee was ratified by all these chiefs, she brought his name before the Great Council of the chiefs of the League, who also approved of her choice.

And so it came that before the corn was gathered in that fall, Glad-tidings was made chief in place of his mother's brother.

XI

Some summers passed and strange rumors began to reach Hanging-flower. First came Full-moon, and in many words told the mother that Glad-tidings was suspected of having made a dishonorable agreement with the Sioux. He had promised, she averred, to exercise his influence with the warriors of his people so that they would not attack the Sioux while the latter were fighting the Algonquin. Then Crossing-of-the-roads came, Fleet-of-foot's brother, and he spoke in grave tones about the dishonor that Glad-tidings' act had brought upon his people. Day after day, men and women came and spoke earnestly and vehemently to Hanging-flower, and the tenor of the news they brought was always the same.

XII

Hanging-flower was pale and haggard now, and from day to day she was losing weight. But one day she felt that she was mother no longer, but the matron of her family. She called on Glad-tidings, the chief, and standing before him, admonished him in ceremonial terms to desist from his shameful ways, which were bringing dishonor upon his people. But should he persist, such were her parting words, she would call on him again, and then once more, accompanied by the Chief Warrior, and then she would depose him and he would be chief no longer.

The days passed and the rumors persisted. Hanging-flower called on Glad-tidings for the second time; and when she had spoken, he said nothing. In a little while, she called on him for the third time, accompanied by the Chief Warrior. As both of them stood facing Glad-tidings, the Chief Warrior said: "I will now admonish you for the last time, and if you continue to resist acceding to and obeying our request, then your duties as chief of our family and clan will cease, and I shall take the deer's horns from off your head, and with a broad strong-edged ax I shall cut the tree down." Having spoken thus, the Chief Warrior "took the deer's horns off Glad-tidings' head," and handed them to Hanging-flower, for from now on Glad-tidings was chief no longer.

Hanging-flower then went to the Council house and informed the other chiefs, in person, that Glad-tidings had been deposed. As she spoke, her heart broke, for she knew that "the coals had gone out on the fire" of her family, and the chieftainship was lost.

A few days after this, Full-moon called on Hanging-flower and informed her in many words that Feathered-arrow, Full-moon's son, was to be chief in Glad-tidings' place and that the chiefs of the League had transferred the chieftainship to her family.

In the evening of that day Hanging-flower, wrapped in a blanket, went outside of the village. For a long time she stood there, on the hill above the cornfields. Her thoughts turned to the past and for a long time she was lost in memories.... But of the future she did not care to think.

Alexander A. Goldenweiser

SLENDER-MAIDEN OF THE APACHE

Slender-maiden was to have her dance in twelve days. The acorns were now ripening along Ash Creek; the stags, their horns fully grown, were taking on fat; thunder-showers were now falling, and the year was at its best. During the preceding spring, Slender-maiden's mother had noted her daughter's approach to womanhood. The winter before, Slender-maiden's father had gone to the mountains beyond Black River and hunted for half a month. The best of the deerskins had been carefully tanned and put away. On Cibicu Creek, a day to the west, lived a man noted for the fine buckskin suits he could make. Slender-maiden's father took four of these dressed deerskins and two of his best horses to this skilled man. The horses were given him for his work on the skins. Slender-maiden's father was told to come for the garments about the time corn showed its tassels.

Slender-maiden's mother and Slender-maiden herself were Wormwood clan. Many women of this clan lived in the neighborhood and they gladly agreed to help gather food for the feast. Slender-maiden's father was of the Adobe clan. His brothers promised to join him before the dance, in a hunt which should provide venison for the feast. There was, fortunately, a large number of horses belonging to the family with which those who sang the songs and directed the ceremony might be paid.

Slender-maiden's father rode up the creek to the marsh where he cut a supply of reeds. Of these he made tubes, which he filled with tobacco and tied at right angles, making crosses. These were sent by Slender-maiden's cousin, a young man but recently with a beard to pluck, to the medicine man living on Eastfork who knew the songs of Naiyenezgani, used for the dance of adolescent girls. When the young man arrived at the home of the singer he placed the cross on his toe. As the old man reached for the token he asked the young man from whence he came.

"I am Wormwood clan and I come from the valley of dancehouse. Slender-maiden's father, my uncle, asks that on the twelfth day you sing for his daughter under the cotton-woods on Ash Creek. He sends you this deerskin, these beads of turquoise, of jet, of white stone, and of red coral. Besides he gives you a horse, and a saddle from Old Mexico."

"Sit, my grandchild," said the singer to the young man. The old man then filled his pipe and passed his buckskin bag of tobacco to the young man. "Call my brothers," he said to his wife before they began smoking. When they had gathered and the pipes were burning, the singer told the young man's errand and that their aid was required in the ceremony. Food was now brought and the young man was served.

A similar invitation was sent to a medicine man on Turkey Creek who knew the dance of the Gans.

A few days later the women of Slender-maiden's clan and those living in her camp loaded their burros and horses with the food for the feast and the necessary utensils. The sun was well up when they were ready to start, and by sundown the party camped when they reached a stream where oaks grew in profusion, about two-thirds of the way to Ash Creek. By noon the next day, camp was made under the cotton-woods in the valley of the creek.

The day before the dance was to be held a sweat lodge was built near the stream. In this dome-shaped lodge, parties of six and eight men went repeatedly for baths. The songs of Naiyenezgani were sung and the men were purified by the steam and heat. At midday, food was served to all those who had gathered in the vicinity.

Just before the sun rose the next morning, four blankets were spread, one above the other, and a cane, bent at the top, was stood up just east of this bed. Near the cane was placed a basket of shelled corn.

The singer from Eastfork with his chorus of young men formed a line just back of the western end of the bed. Slender-maiden now appeared and took her place in front of the singers, facing the rising sun. As the songs were sung in proper order Slender-maiden danced, swaying her body from side to side. When the proper song was reached, she knelt and moved from side to side on alternate knees with her face always toward the rising sun. Soon she lay prone on the bed and was molded to a form of beauty by her matronly attendant. Finally she was prayed for by all the assembled spectators who passed in line behind her and put pollen on the crown of her head. When the sun was about halfway to the middle of the sky she ran the appointed race and the morning ceremony was completed. Every one was soon served with meat and soup.

That evening at about sunset a man without clothes, except a breech-cloth, his body painted white with black stripes, appeared at the dance-ground and by signs inquired if a dance were in progress. On being told that was the case he ran away to a secluded spot. Soon peculiar noises were heard and the sound of rattles. Four men came in single file followed by a painted clown. The four wore moccasins and kilts below the waist but were painted black above with symbolic designs in white. Their faces were covered and on the tops of their heads were fan-shaped forms of wood covered with painted designs. After making a circuit of the dance-ground, these masked men danced for some time and then withdrew.

After nightfall a great fire was kindled and the masked men returned. Slender-maiden, bearing her cane, danced near the fire. With her were other maidens who occasionally invited young men to dance with them. While the masked men were dancing, the singer from Turkey Creek led the songs of the Gans, immortals who join with men in the celebration of attaining adolescence. The time of the songs was marked by the singers beating on a stretched skin.

When the earth was made,
When the sky was made,
Where the head of the black earth lies,
Where the head of the black sky lies,
Where the heads of them meet,
Black Thunder, Black Gan, facing each other with life stepped out.
Black Gan with his dance spoke four times.

About midnight the singer from Eastfork and his assistants took their places within a house consisting of four poles only. A fire was kindled here, back of which, facing the east, stood Slender-maiden accompanied by a girl of her own age, and two youths. At intervals until dawn the songs of Naiyenezgani were sung while the young people danced.

Estsunnadlehe
From her house of white cloud
Living white shell, her chief,
It echoes with me.

Estsunnadlehe
Long and fortunate life, her chief,
It echoes with me.

After breakfast more songs were sung and then the masked men
appeared and assisted, first in painting Slender-maiden with white
earth and later in marking with symbols the cheeks and hands of all the
spectators. The ceremony was now complete and the assembly soon dis-
persed, some people to the gathering of acorns and some to their camps
in order to tend their crops.

Among those who had been at the ceremony at Ash Creek was a
young man named Red-boy. His home was on San Pedro Creek, one
hundred miles south and west, not far from the country of the Pima. He
had come to visit relatives in the White Mountain country for his mother
was of the Adobe clan and her brothers and sisters were living on the
White River.

Red-boy was much interested in Slender-maiden and resolved to seek
her for a wife. His request was listened to, and his presents of horses
were accepted. Slender-maiden herself was pleased, for the stranger was
tall, and generous with his presents to her. The couple soon moved to a
camp on Black River, where Slender-maiden was left behind while her
husband joined a small party which was going to Mexico on a raid. Ten
days later the party returned without loss and with a large number of
horses. Red-boy had taken ten which he gave Slender-maiden's parents.

The next spring Red-boy and Slender-maiden went to the village on
San Pedro and planted the land that had belonged to Red-boy's mother.
Here they lived for five years, raising good crops and having plenty of
deer from the surrounding mountains.

One day in August Slender-maiden and her sister-in-law were
making baskets under the cotton-woods by the creek. Slender-maiden's
five-year old daughter was sleeping under a willow nearer the stream
where the breeze was cooler. Suddenly a roar was heard and a wall of
water, mud, and torn-up trees rushed out of the canyon. The women
jumped up, but before they could reach the sleeping child the water had
rolled over in a brown flood. The women themselves were able to escape
by climbing into the cotton-woods.

Saddened by this loss and disconcerted by the washing over of the
farm by the waters of a thunder-shower, Slender-maiden and her hus-

band moved to the White Mountain country and settled on Cedar Creek near her people. Here they lived for ten years. There were now five children, the youngest of which was a girl.

One day a messenger came from White River asking that Slender-maiden's husband come to treat a sick man. Red-boy knew the songs and ritual of a healing ceremony. He went with his wife, and camped by the man who had been suddenly taken ill. He was burning with fever and covered with an eruption. The songs were of no avail for before dawn the man was dead. The body was almost immediately placed in a cleft of the rocks in a nearby canyon and covered with sticks and stones.

That afternoon Slender-maiden and her husband moved down White River and a few days later to Black River in which she and her husband bathed. That night her head ached and she begged her husband to leave, lest he too contract the disease. When twelve days later the fever left her, she saw her husband sitting by, tired and worn with watching over her.

"Why did you not leave me?" she asked.

"Because I have loved you for many years," he replied.

In a few days he too was ill and then Slender-maiden, still weak, watched him until he was taken to the canyon for burial. When the plague had passed, Slender-maiden's children and near relatives were all dead except the youngest girl who had been left with an aunt on Cedar Creek.

Slender-maiden cut her hair, of course, and wore only a skirt and a poncho of cloth. Even when the year was up she did not allow her hair to grow. Her husband's clansmen, noting her disinclination to marry again, respected her wishes and did not assign her a husband. She continued the cultivation of her small farm and the care of her daughter.

The requests of her adolescence ceremony for long life were answered. So old is she that she must walk with a cane. Her hair is white, not with the symbolic white earth but with age. Her daughter, in middle age, unmarried, highly respected, but much sought for herself and her considerable herds, attends to her physical needs. For the remainder, Slender-maiden lives with her memories of a happy youth.

P. E. Goddard

EARTH-TONGUE, A MOHAVE

Earth-tongue's earliest recollection was of the dim, cool house, where he picked bits of charcoal out of the soft sand and crumbled it against his hand. Once a cricket appeared on the wattled wall, suddenly went back in when he thrust at it, and only a stream of dry soil sifted forth. And then there was the terrifying time when voices burst loudly into his sleep, people crowded in but stood helplessly awkward, while his father's brother shot insults of stolid hate into the ceaseless flood of his wife's vituperation. As the woman turned to beat a girl lurking in the corner and the man interposed and flung her off, Earth-tongue burst into bawling and clung to his mother. He saw the angry woman stamp on pot after pot, tear open her coils of shredded bark and strew them into the fire, and then, suddenly silent, load her belongings into a carrying-frame and stagger out. The frame caught in the door: as she tore it through, the contents crashed, and a laugh rose in the house; but Earth-tongue sobbed long.

He was larger when he paddled with other children at the edge of the slough; but still very small as he first remembered himself seeing the great, stretching river that drew by with mysterious, swirling noises in its red eddies. He and his little brother were put into a huge pot which his father and another man pushed before them across stream: their hair as it coiled high on their heads was just visible over the edge as they swam. And then followed an interminable trudge somewhere through the dust, relieved only by rides on his father's back, and on his grandmother.

He was older when he shot his first bow; when at dusk he caught a woodpecker in its hole and would not let go though it hacked desperately at his clasped hands, until a half-grown cousin took it from him to imprison under a turned jar for the night. His father wove a cage the next day, and the captive was installed, but remained wild, and one

X2144-07

morning was dead. And then came the time when the boys of Mesquite-water challenged those of his settlement on a hot, summer day after the inundation had half dried, and they slung lumps of mud at each other from the ends of long willow poles. There were other events that must have fallen soon after this period, but which he did not remember: when he rolled his hair into long, slim cylinders, began to measure how nearly it reached his hip, and made his first advances to girls.

Even before this he had dreamed of Mastamho, gigantic on the peak Avikwa'me in the great, dark, round house full of peoples; of the two Ravens singing of dust whirls and war and of the far away clumps of cane waiting to be cut into flutes; and of the river, drawn from its source to wash away the ashes and bones of Matavilya where the pinnacles stand in the gorge at House-post-water. He knew later that he had dreamed these things as a little boy, even while he was still in his mother; he did not yet think about them, except when the old man his grandfather, and his father and uncles, sang of them.

One day a runner came up the valley and shouted pantingly that strangers had appeared from the east at dawn and killed a woman and two children at Sand-back, besides wounding a man and his younger brother. The men leaped for their weapons; the women called in their children, loaded themselves with property, and soon began to track northward in a straggling, excited stream. Earth-tongue pulled down his bow and raked among the roof thatch for such arrows as he could assemble. Then he joined his kinsmen and male neighbors who stood in a group in front of one of the shades, exclaiming and pointing at a smoke that rose down the valley. Bundles of crude, blunt arrows projected behind their hips, shoved under cord belts; and many had clubs dangling from their wrists. Earth-tongue did not own a club: he had never seen battle; and he hung about the outside of the cluster of seasoned men.

Soon, refugees from the nearer settlements began to arrive; and then a body of fighting men from up the valley, bedaubed for war.

Earth-tongue's kinsmen merged with them; and as they proceeded south, growing in numbers, they met ever more women and children, and finally those from the point of attack, until, not far away in the cotton-woods, they came upon the men of Sand-back. The enemy were Halchidhoma from far down-stream, they were now informed, not Wal-apai as at first conjectured. They had avoided the river, traversing the

desert to hide in the Walapai mountains and descend at night upon the nearer tip of the Mohave land. They had long since gone off—sixty they were said to number, as they were seen to file over the rocks far above the stream at Pinnacles. They had looted and burnt only the group of houses at Sand-back, killed the woman, and lightly wounded with an arrow one of the men who fought back from a distance: the other reported casualties turned up safe. But the enemy had carried off the woman's head, and would dance about its skin. Earth-tongue gazed at the collapsed houses, their charred posts smoking on the mass of sand; and that night he watched the beheaded woman's cremation. There was much talk of retaliation, but an immediate attack would have found the Halchidhoma prepared or perhaps removed.

So some months elapsed without a move being made; and meanwhile Earth-tongue became married. In the turmoil of the Halchidhoma invasion, as party after party trooped by, he had been attracted by the sight of a girl, barely but definitely passed out of childhood, and only a little younger than himself, who halted, leaning under her laden carrying-frame, behind her mother, as their group paused for an excited colloquy. He saw that the girl noted his eyes on her and glanced away, and he knew, from the people she was with, that her name was Kata. Not long after, he began to find errands or companions that took him to her settlement. Soon a mutual familiarity of each other's presence was established, the purport of which was manifest even though direct speech between the two young people was infrequent and brief. Both were shy; until one afternoon a blind old man, the girl's father's uncle, who knew of Earth-tongue's repeated presence from the references of the family, addressed him and her directly. "Why do you not marry?" he said. "Persons do not live long. Soon you will be old like myself, unable to please yourselves. It is good that you sleep and play together. You, young man, should stay here the night." Neither Earth-tongue nor the girl answered. But he remained through the evening meal and after; and when the house was dark, went silently to where she lay. The next day, he stayed on; the day after, returned briefly to his home; and from then on, spent increasing time at his new abode, where, without a word having been spoken, he slipped into a more and more recognized status. He did not work, unless special occasion called, such as assisting with a seine-net; and Kata only occasionally helped her relatives farm. Instead, they spent much time together, lolling under the shade, toying or teasing each other, or listening to their elders. Sometimes he sang softly as he lay by her, or she bent over him searching his head or untangling his clustered locks, or tried to draw the occasional hairs from his face with her teeth; and ever she laughed more freely. So the days followed one another.

When at last the Mohave were ready, it was announced that they would once for all destroy the Halchidhoma. The entire nation was to move and appropriate the enemy land. Soon they started, most of the men in advance, weaponed and unburdened save for gourds of maize meal at their hips; water they did not have to carry since they followed the river. Behind tramped the women, children, and old men, under loads. Foods, blankets of bark and rabbit fur, fish nets, metates, household property, and the most necessary pottery vessels were taken. The remainder of their belongings and stored provisions were buried or hidden away: every house in the valley stood empty.

For five days they walked. Then the men suddenly surrounded a group of settlements. These were the houses of the Kohuana, a far downstream tribe, wasted by wars with their neighbors, until the pressed remnant had sought refuge half a day's journey above the Halchidhoma to whom they were united, less by positive friendship than by common foes and parallel fortunes. For the Halchidhoma, too, remembered having once lived populously among the welter of tribes in the broad bottom lands below the mouth of the Gila. With the Kohuana the Mohave had no direct quarrel; and though they arrived armed and overpowering, they proclaimed themselves kinsmen, and anounced that they had come as guests. By night the Kohuana houses overflowed with the mob of Mohave families. Kohuana messengers were dispatched to summon the Halchidhoma to battle at White-spread-rock-place, if they were not afraid. Such challenge the outnumbered people could not find it in their manhood to evade. So the next day saw them in line at the appointed field, barely a hundred strong, against perhaps four hundred that the Mohave mustered after setting a guard over their families.

Earth-tongue went into battle with much inward excitement, but little fear, and listened obediently to the admonitions of his seasoned kinsmen. Even before arrows could reach, the shooting began. Before long, arrows flew feebly by, and then it became necessary to twist sharply sidewise to avoid them. At this distance the two lines shot at each oth-

er, taunting and leaping, while, in the rear, half-grown boys and a few old men helped to gather up and replenish bundles of arrows. What the Halchidhoma lacked in frequency of shots, they partly made up in greater openness of target; and before long, struck men began to withdraw temporarily on each side. The Mohave could have made short work by charging in a body with their clubs; but they had asked for an open stand-up fight, and besides found pleasure in the game, which fell increasingly to their advantage. For hours they sweated in the sun, gradually and irregularly forcing the Halchidhoma line back, and shouting whenever one of the foe was carried off.

At last the leaders called that it was time to cease, and defied the foe to resume in the same spot on the fourth day. Then they trooped victoriously home, without a fatality, though a few, weakened from bleeding or with parts of shafts broken off in them, were carried on the backs of companions. Earth-tongue had been struck twice. One arrow had grazed the skin of his flank when he became overconfident and failed to bend his body with sudden enough vigor. Then, one of three shafts that came toward him almost at once had imbedded itself a finger-joint's depth in the front of his thigh, and hung there until he hastily plucked it out. Neither wound bled profusely, especially after a bit of charcoal was reached him to rub in for stanching; and he returned stiff, tired, and proud. The Halchidhoma losses were severer. None of them appeared to have fallen dead on the field; but at least half had been struck, and a number so vitally or often that they would die.

For four days the Mohave treated their wounds, talked of the next battle, and ate their hosts' provisions. Then they set out. But the Halchidhoma had sent their families down-stream and taken up a new stand farther back. Here they joined once more, and the fight went on as before but with ever more preponderance to the Mohave, until these, wearied by the noon sun, contemptuously drew off to the river to drink. The Halchidhoma seized the occasion to run to their children and women, set these across the river, and strike east over the desert. When the victors reappeared, the fugitives were far. The Mohave thereupon decided to occupy their fields and houses until the dispossessed might come to drive them out; which the latter, by this time safely received among the Maricopa far across the desert on the Gila, had no intention of doing. However, the Mohave lived nearly a year in the land of the

Halchidhoma, adjusting themselves as they could; and returned only as the next flood and planting time approached, taking the Kohuana along to settle among themselves, where these enforced visitors remained for some years.

Before the stay in the Halchidhoma country was over, Earth-tongue and Kata had drifted apart. The derangement of accustomed residence, enforced with others, Earth-tongue's pride as an incipient warrior, the fact that no child was born, all contributed to separate them increasingly. Each formed new interests while vaguely jealous of the other's; and in the end Earth-tongue brought not Kata but another girl to his parents' house.

Soon after his first child was born—a daughter, called Owich like the sisters of himself, his father, and his father's father—Earth-tongue grew restless for adventure, and, the time being one of peace, joined himself to those that would travel. Ten or twenty in number, they would go out: too few to excite apprehension of treacherous intent, too many to be made away with safely. Each carried maize, water, his weapons, and whatever he might wish to trade. On shorter journeys they prided themselves on being able to travel at a trot four days without food, and with only such drink as the desert might afford, chewing perhaps a bit of willow as a relief for the dryness of their mouths. But these hardships they underwent mostly in emulation, or toward the last of a return with Mohave land before them. Again and again Earth-tongue went down the river, through Yuma, Kamia, Halyikwamai, and Cocopa settlements, to the flat shores of the salt sea; east into the Walapai mountains and down into the chasm of the Havasupai, where he saw strange-speaking and strangely dressed Hopi and Navaho, heard of their stone towns, and brought home their belts and, once, a blanket of white cotton.

To the northwest he visited the Chemehuevi and other Paiutes about their scattered springs, and ate their foods of seeds and wild fruits, some familiar, some strange; and mescal and sometimes deer.

Theirs was a strange language too, but he had heard a little from the few Chemehuevi who lived at the northern extreme of Mohave valley and beyond it on Cotton-wood island; and many of his companions could speak more. They went from Paiute band to band, to where the river no longer flows from the north but from the east, beyond the Muddy, and found each group like the last in customs, but of new foods.

They listened to the stories of the Paiute, who dreamed of the mountain Niivant as the Mohave do of Aikwa'me, and to whom they sang their songs, which the Paiute wished to hear.

To the west were many tribes, all different tongued, but mostly easy to understand a little when one knew Chemehuevi. There were the Vanyume on their river that dried into nothing and left them always half-starved; the Hanyuvecha in the range of great pines beyond; northward, about Three-Mountains, the Kuvahye, adjoined by other mountaineers, little tribes, unwarlike, friendly to the visitors, some of whom they hailed as old friends. They offered no smoke, but gave tobacco crushed in a mortar with shells; which Earth-tongue and his companions ate in courtesy, and were nearly all made to sweat and vomit violently thereby. From a crest near here they looked over a vast plain beyond, in which shimmered what one of his companions said were large lakes. He had been there and seen the people, who lived in long houses of rushes—a hundred fires in line within one house—and ate rush roots, and slept on rushes, and at night worms came up and troubled the sleepers. And in the tumbled range on which they stood, but beyond them, were the Like Mohave, a very little like them in speech, but naked, unkempt, and poor. Them Earth-tongue saw, but not in their own houses.

And going out again, he traversed the land of the tribes to the south-west, unfriendly, half-sullen, and dangerous to small parties. The Hakwicha dug wells and ate mesquite; beyond them were people in the mountains, about hot springs, who sang to turtle shells instead of gourds; and still farther, stretching down to the ocean that one could see from their peaks, lived the Foreign-Kamia, speaking almost like the real Kamia, but knowing nothing of farmed foods, eating rattle-snakes, and a hostile lot to venture among. They had some grudges to pay off to the Mohave for plundered settlements, but were not a people to travel far from their homes even for revenge.

The Yavapai, too, Earth-tongue came to know, though theirs was not an attractive country to visit. They dreamed and sang like the Mohave, but of other animals; and some of their stories were the same. Their neighbors and friends were the Roaming-Yavapai, a small-statured, sharp-eyed people, wearing their hair flowing, fierce lance fighters, taciturn, violent, untrustworthy; but inclined favorably to the Mohave in spite of the utter unintelligibility of their speech because they knew them through the Yavapai as traditionally hostile, like themselves, against the Maricopa and that people of innumerable houses, the Pima. These last Earth-tongue never came to know save on the field of battle.

One early summer, as the river was flooding, its rise suddenly stopped. The inundation being wont to grow in interrupted stages the people waited quietly for its resumption. But the water fell back and back. Then some began to declare that it might not rise again, and advised planting at once before the moist ground should dry: but others pointed out that high water was yet due, and had often come late, and that present planting in that case would cause the seed to wash out and be lost. So nearly all waited with concern and much discussing; until finally the river was wholly back within its banks and dropping decisively. Then they knew that nothing more was to be hoped for that season, and men and women hastened to save what they might of the crop. But many of the fields had remained untouched by water, and most of the others were already half dry. In some, the maize and beans never sprouted; in some they came up indeed, but soon wilted; and though the women carried water in jars, only small patches could be effectively served in this hand fashion.

Soon, every one knew that famine impended, and that so few houses would grow even enough harvest for another seeding, that the year after would also be hard to survive. They gathered every wisp of wild seed plants in the uncultivated bottoms; but these wild seeds, too, had come up thin, and the crop of mesquite pods was pitiful.

The women labored faithfully, and the children watched over the scattered maize; yet though the grain ripened, the scattered stalks were too few to keep any house through the winter. Some families did not pick even an ear. A moon after harvest time, the crop was consumed; by winter, the last of the other stores. The men fished daily, but the sloughs and ponds had never filled and were soon seined out, and the river's yield was uncertain and far insufficient. Every one was gaunt; the children lay listlessly about; sickness grew. Earth-tongue's wife, and his older brother's, had planted with his mother in his father's ancestral field, which lay low and was long-proved rich. So they fared better than many. Nevertheless, before spring the emaciated bodies of two children and an old woman had been burnt and Earth-tongue had three times sung himself hoarse as they lay dying.

The young men went out with their bows, and now and then re-

turned with a bird or gopher or badger, but oftener empty-handed. People who had new belongings went to the Walapai to trade for mescal and deer meat. Whole families trudged to visit the Chemehuevi, until they brought back word that these hosts too were eaten out. At last not a day passed without columns of smoke from pyres visible somewhere in the valley. It was a terrible year and long remembered before the end of another summer brought partial abatement.

So numerous had been the deaths from bowel flux and cough, that shaman after shaman fell a victim to the anger of the kin of those he had attempted to save. Yellow-thigh, a powerful man and not very old, had lost two patients during the famine, and three more at intervals since. Mutterings were frequent; but no one had found opportunity, or dared, to work vengeance on him. One morning, Earth-tongue and a friend, sauntering up valley on some errand, turned to a house before which Yellow-thigh lay, for those there were kinsmen of his. No men were about; and as the two visitors stood in the door, his friend on sudden impulse whispered to Earth-tongue, "Let us kill him." So they sat down for a little and passed the news of the day, then arose, Earth-tongue reaching for his bow and four cross-pointed arrows, with the remark that they were going to shoot doves. The shaman grunted assent and the pair passed out.

For a time they traversed the brush, planning the deed. At the mesa edge they broke two stones to sharp edges, and then returned. Yellow-thigh lay under the shade-roof with closed eyes, breathing regularly. The friend went by him to look into the house, and finding it empty, nodded. Earth-tongue, who had approached, bent suddenly down and struck with all his might at the sleeper's head.

The shaman pushed himself to a sitting position as the blood began to pour from the mangled side of his face. The friend started back, then plunged forward to finish the man, and swung; but his excited arm brought the weapon down only on the victim's knee. Then he staggered off, scarcely able in fright and emotion to drag his own legs. Earth-tongue, seeing the shaman still sitting, strode forward again and with both hands drove the point of the stone through the top of his skull. Two women who had been going through each other's hair in the shadow of the brush fence outside, half turned at the noise and shrieked, while Earth-tongue dashed after his companion, seized his hand, and dragged

him forward. They ran through the willows and at last lay down to pant in hiding; and here, after they had quieted, Earth-tongue laughed at his friend's faltering stroke and steps. Then they went on, still keeping to cover, until around the second bend they swam the river.

On the other side, old men were gaming with poles and hoop, and others watched. The two sat down and looked on. Three times, four times, until it was early afternoon, the players bet and threw their poles and one or the other finally took up the stakes. Then Earth-tongue said, "I have killed a shaman, the large man at Sloping-gravel."

"Yes, kill him," answered one of the old men, thinking he was boasting of an empty intent; and a spectator added, "Indeed, it would be well. Too many persons are dying."

"I have killed him," Earth-tongue said again, and they began to believe him. So they went to the houses. Soon word came that the shaman was dead; and then his kinsmen arrived, angry and threatening, and accusations flew back and forth, while Earth-tongue stood unmoved and silent but wary. The kinsmen finally challenged to a stick fight the next day, and withdrew to burn the dead man.

The people of the settlement commended Earth-tongue and promised to engage for him; and in the morning they and all his kin and the kin of those whom the shaman had brought to their death, gathered in the center of a large playing field. Each man carried a willow as thick as his forearm and reaching to his neck; and in his left hand, a shorter parrying stick. The challengers appeared, somewhat fewer in number and with tear-marked faces, but enraging their opponents by crying the names of their dead parents and grandparents. Then the two bodies, spreading into irregular lines, rushed at each other. Each man swung at an antagonist's head, now with his staff held in one hand, now in both. Blows beat down on heads through the guard, rained on shoulders, bruised knuckles, and the willows clashed amid the shouts. Now and then a staff broke and a contestant ran back to seize a new one. The fighters sweated, panted, rubbed blood out of their eyes and staggered forward and back as the lines swayed in the clamor. Once or twice a maddened fighter, running in under his opponent's strokes, seized his hair to belabor him with his parry-club; whereupon shouts of "Bad, bad! no! no! release!" arose and a multitude of rescuers' blows drove him back. The shaman's side were getting the worst of it, but rallied again and again without being driven wholly to their end of the field. Strokes became fewer and feebler. Weary arms could no longer rise. Fighter after fighter leaned on his stick, or sat on the ground in the rear. Each side taunted the other to come on again; and at last they drew apart, every man panting, bruised, and weary, but satisfied at the damage he had inflicted. No heads had been broken and no one died, though some were sick for a few days from maggots that had bred in the scalp under their clotted hair; and then talk died down and the enmity gradually subsided. Earth-tongue won the praise of all the Mohave who were not directly involved.

Once, runners came from the Yuma to invite to an attack on the Cocopa at the mouth of the river. A hundred and twenty Mohave went down. The kohota or play-chief of the northern Mohave asked for captives, although he already had several; and Earth-tongue was one of the men whom he requested to carry food and water for the prisoner's return journey, and to guard against their escape.

The Yuma contingent was even larger than the Mohave one; and the attack was made at daybreak. It was not much of a fight. The first house entered gave the alarm and the settlement scattered amid yells. Only two Cocopa were killed by the Yuma and two young women, sisters, called Night-hawk, captured by the Mohave. The latter stayed with the Yuma four days to watch the scalp dance; but no one of them having touched the corpses, they were not in need of purification, and returned home.

The whole tribe came out to escort them to the kohota's house.

There the captives were made to sit down, while the kohota stood up and sang Pleiades. Then men and women, facing each other, danced. When the sun was at its height, they stopped, ate what the kohota's women brought out, then lay in the shade or gambled. In the afternoon the kohota called out a Chutaha singer. Soon the sounding jar began to boom, the people left off their play, and danced: three rows of young men with feathers tied in their hair, one row of old men, and two women standing separate. Then at last, as the sun was coming low, the chief came with rattles in his hand and at the end of a song shouted: "Let him sing who wishes to! Let any woman sing! I appoint no one!" Women grasped the rattles and carried them, one to a Tumanpa singer, others to those who knew Vinimulya and Vinimulya-hapacha; and one was brought to Earth-tongue to sing Raven. Soon all four of the dance series were in

progress at different places, while those women who liked Nyohaiva, having persuaded an old man to sing that, began to revolve about him standing shoulder to shoulder. As fast as one song ended, the singers took up another, for the sun had nearly set, and the sweating women clamored for more, while the crowd of people stood about.

With darkness they stopped to bathe and eat and rest, then danced again, singing as before and new kinds too, while off on the side, by the light of a fire, groups of men played hiding game to the Tudhulva songs through the night. In the morning the kohota had the assemblage bathe, fed them once more, and sent them home to return two days later.

This time they danced again all evening, all afternoon, and all night. As the sun rose, the kohota, still singing, took the two captives one by each hand, and walked toward the river. Behind him came the Tumanpa and Vinimulya singers, each with his crowd, and then the mass of people in procession. The kohota, still holding the two girls, ran over the bank, and every one followed. This made Mohaves of the captives, and people were no longer afraid of them.

The kohota led them back to his house, where they were to live, and said, "Perhaps these girls will marry and bear children, who, belonging to both tribes, will make peace when they grow up, and there will be no more war." So it came in part. After two years, one of the sisters married, and soon had a child. The other continued without husband. In time, formal peace was made between the Yuma and Cocopa; whereupon the kohota announced, "Since the tribes are friends now, let us not keep Night-hawk longer." So a party led her to the Yuma, where her kinsmen met and escorted her home. Her sister remained with her Mohave husband.

Earth-tongue was beginning to grow old. His oldest son and one daughter both had children, and his hair showed first streaks of gray. He thought more of his youth, and commenced to remember what he had dreamed then. He knew he had seen Matavilya sick and gradually dying and burned, and his ashes washed away by the river that Mastamho made to flow out of the ground. He remembered too Mastamho's house on Avikwa'me, with the multitudes inside it in rows like little children, and Mastamho instructing them; and how he repeated after him, correctly, until Mastamho said to him, "That is right! You know it! You have it! I gave it to you!" Then he had dreamed how Sky-rattle-snake was at last inveigled from his house far in the south ocean, and his head cut off on Avikwa'me. Earth-tongue saw his joints and blood and sweat and juices turn into eggs. From these eggs hatched Rattle-snake, Spider, Scorpion, and Yellow-ant, who went off to Three-Mountains and remote places, deep in the earth or high in the sky, and from there built four roads to all tribes. When they wish a man for a friend, they bite him and take his shadow home with them. "But another road leads from their house to my heart," Earth-tongue would say, "and I know what they do. And I intercept the shadow before Rattle-snake has led it wholly to Three-Mountains, and sing it back; I break the roads of spittle that Spider has begun to wind four times around the man's heart; and so he lives again."

Then Earth-tongue commenced to be sent for when people were bitten—first his relatives, then others. He would stand up at once and sing to bring a cooling wind; and, reaching the sick person, sing over him from the north, west, south, and east, but not a fifth time, lest he die. Then, sending every one away but a wife or mother, and forbidding all drink, he would sit by the patient all night, singing his four songs from time to time. In the morning the sick person used to get up well.

Fighting interrupted these pursuits. It was a summons again from the Yuma, this time against the Maricopa; and two hundred of the Mohave responded. The seventh night they were on Maricopa soil and met eighty Yuma by appointment; and in the morning advanced to attack. But the Maricopa had got wind of their presence, and when the fight opened were re-enforced by a vast number of the Pima. The Mohave and Yuma exhorted one another, and though man after man fell, gave ground slowly, fighting back outnumbered. At last the enemy ran all in a body against them. Part of the Mohave broke before the shock and fled to the north, ultimately escaping. But sixty of them formed with the Yuma on a little knoll near the Gila, where they stood in a dense mass. As the Pima and Maricopa dashed against them, they dragged man after man struggling into their midst, where he was dispatched with fierce club blows on his head or thrusts into his face. Twice, Earth-tongue leaped out to grasp an opponent and fling him over his back, thus protecting his own skull, while his companions beat the struggling foe to death. The fighting grew wilder. The Pima no longer drew back to shoot but swirled incessantly

around and into the dwindling cluster at bay. At last the shouts ceased; the dust began to settle; and all but two of the Yuma, and every man of the sixty Mohave, lay with crushed head or mangled body on foreign earth.

A. L. Kroeber

Sayach'apis, a Nootka Trader

Tom is a blind old man, whose staff may be heard any day stumping or splashing along the village street of his tribal reservation, or up or down the hillside that slopes to the smoke-drying huts massed by the Somass river. He is an honored member of the Ts'isha'ath, a Nootka tribe that is now permanently located a few miles up from the head of Alberni Canal, the deepest inlet on the west coast of Vancouver Island. The Ts'isha'ath fishes and harpoons along the river, the length of the "Canal," and down among the hundreds of islands that dot Barkley Sound, the first of the large bays north of Cape Beale that are carved out on the stormy coast line of the island.

Tom's early life was passed at the now abandoned village of Hik-wis, whose row of houses looked out upon the main water of the Sound, but for decades he has led an uneventful existence in his river reservation and its vicinity, old summer fishing-grounds that were conquered in the first instance by his people from an alien tribe. Within convenient reach are the slowly booming white men's towns of Alberni and Port Alberni, where one may lay in a supply of biscuits and oranges for a tribal feast, or make periodic complaint to the Indian Agent. Tom is now old and poverty-stricken, but the memory of his former wealth is with his people. The many feasts he has given and the many ceremonial dances and displays he has had performed have all had their desired effect—they have shed luster on his sons and daughters and grandchildren, they have "put his family high" among the Ts'isha'ath tribe, and they have even carried his name to other, distant Nootka tribes, and to tribes on the east coast of the island that are of alien speech. Nowadays he spends much of his time by the fireside, tapping his staff in accompaniment to old ritual tunes that he is never tired of humming.

Tom's present name is Sayach'apis, Stands-up-high-over-all. It is an old man's name of eight generations' standing, that hails from the Hisawist'ath, a now extinct Nootka tribe with which Tom is connected through his father's mother's mother, who was herself a Hisawist'ath on her mother's side. The tribe is extinct, but its personal names, like its songs and legends and distinctive ritualistic ceremonies, linger on among the neighboring tribes through the fine spun network of inheritance. The name "Stands-up-high-overall," like practically all Nootka, and indeed all West Coast names, has its legendary background, its own historical warrant. The first Nootka chief to bear the name, obtained it in a dream. He was undergoing ritualistic training in the woods in the pursuit of "power" for the attainment of wealth, and had not slept for a long time. At last he fell into a heavy slumber, and this is what he dreamed: The Sky Chief appeared to him and said, "Why are you sleeping, Stands-up-high-over-all? You are not really desirous of getting wealthy, are you? I was about to make you wealthy and to give you the name Stands-up-high-over-all." The ironical touch is a characteristic nuance in these origin legends. And so the name, a supernatural gift, was handed down the generations, now by direct male inheritance, now as a dower to a son-in-law, resident at some village remote from its place of origin. This is the normal manner, actually or in theory, of the transmission of all privileges, and though the owner of a privilege may be a villager a hundred miles or more distant from its historical or legendary home, he has not completely established his right to its use unless he has shown himself, directly or by reference to a speaker acquainted with tribal lore, possessed of the origin legend, the local provenance, and the genealogical tree or "historical" nexus that binds him to the individual, that is believed to have been the first to enjoy the privilege.

Tom did not always have the name of Sayach'apis, nor need he keep it to the end of his days. He assumed it over thirty years ago on the occasion of his great potlatch, a puberty feast in honor of his now deceased oldest daughter. At that time he had the young man's name of Nawe'ik, now borne by his oldest son, Douglas. It is a name belonging to the Nash'as'ath sept or tribal subdivision of the Ts'isha'ath, and was first dreamt by Tom's maternal grandfather. It is thus a name of comparatively recent origin, nor does it possess that aura of noble association that attaches to Tom's present name. Its exact meaning is unknown, but it is said to have been a command—"Come here!"—of a spirit whale, dreamt of by its first possessor. Tom assumed it at a potlatch he gave to his own tribe when he was not yet married. It was just about the time that the discovery of placer gold in the Frazer river was bringing a considerable influx of whites to British Columbia.

Before this, Tom was known as Kunnuh, a Nitinat young man's name, "Wake up!", which is again based on the dream of a spirit whale. The Nitinat Indians are a group of Nootka tribes that occupy the southwest coast of the island, and Tom's claim to the name and to other Nitinat privileges comes to him through his paternal grandfather, himself a Nitinat Indian. The name originated with his grandfather's father's father's father, who received it in a dream as he was training for "power" in whaling. It was assumed by Tom when he was about ten years of age, at a naming feast given the Ts'isha'ath Indians by his Nitinat grandfather. It displaced the boy's name Ha'wihlkumuktli, "Having-chiefs-behind," this time of true Ts'isha'ath origin and descending to Tom through his paternal grandmother's father's father, who again received the name in a dream from a spirit whale. This ancestor was having much success in whaling and, becoming exceedingly wealthy, was "leaving other chiefs behind him." Tom was given the name at an ordinary feast by his paternal grandfather.

The earliest name that Tom remembers having is Tl'i'nitsawa, "Getting-whale-skin." When the great chief Hohenikwop had his whale booty towed to shore, the little boys used to come to the beach for slices of whale skin, so he made up the name of "Getting-whale-skin" for his son. The right to use it was inherited by his oldest son, but was also passed on to the chief's younger sister, who brought it as a dowry to the father of Tom's paternal grandfather. Tom himself received the name on the occasion of a mourning potlatch given by his paternal grandfather in honor of his son, Tom's father, who had died not long before. Before this, Tom had a child's nickname, in other words, a name bestowed not out of the inherited stock of names claimed by his parents, but created on the spot for any chance reason whatever. Such nicknames have no ceremonial value, are not privileges, and are therefore not handed down as an inheritance or transferred as a dowry. Tom has forgotten what his nickname was.

At the very outset, in the mere consideration of what Tom has called himself at various times, we are introduced to the two great social forces

that give atmosphere to Nootka life. The first of these is privilege, the right to something of value, practical or ceremonial. Such a privilege is called "topati" by the Indians, and one cannot penetrate very far into their life or beliefs without stumbling upon one topati after another. The second is the network of descent and kinship relation that determines the status of the North West Coast Indian, not merely as a tribesman once for all, but in reference to his claim to share in any activity of moment. The threads of the genealogical past are wound tightly about the North West Coastman; he is himself a traditional composite of social features that belong to diverse localities, and involve him in diverse kinship relations.

As far back, then, as he can remember, Tom has been steeped in an atmosphere of privilege, of rank, of conflicting claims to this or that coveted right. As far back as he can remember, he has heard remarks like this: "Old man Tootooch has no right to have such and such a particular Thunder-bird dance performed at his potlatches. His claim to it is not clear. In my grandfather's days men were killed for less than that, and the head chief of the Ahous'ath tribe, who has the primary claim to the dance, would have called him sharply to order." But he has also heard Tootooch vigorously support his claim with arguments, genealogical and other, that no one quite knows the right or wrong of. And as far back as he can remember, Tom has been accustomed to think of himself not merely as a Ts'isha'ath, though he is primarily that by residence and immediate descent, but as a participant in the traditions, in the social atmosphere, of several other Nootka tribes. He has always known where to look for his remoter kinsmen, dwelling in villages that are dotted here and there on a long coast line.

The first few years of Tom's life were spent in a "cradle" of basketry, in which he was tightly swathed by sundry wrappings and braids of the soft, beaten inner bark of the cedar. Even now he has a vague recollection of looking out over the sea from the erect vantage of a cradling basket, looped behind his mother's shoulders.

He also thinks he remembers crying bitterly one time when left all by himself in the basket, stood up on end against the butt of a willow tree, while his mother and four or five other women had strayed off to dig for edible clover roots with their hard, pointed digging-sticks. During the cradling period, Tom was having his head, or rather his forehead, gradually flattened by means of cedar-bark pads, and the upper and lower parts of his legs were bandaged so as to allow the calves to bulge. The Indians believe that they do not like big foreheads and slim legs, nor do they approve of wide eyebrows, which are narrowed, if necessary, by plucking out some of the hairs. Later on in life Tom was less particular about his natural appearance, having been well "fixed" by his mother in infancy. Like the other men of his tribe, he has never bothered to pluck out the scanty growth of hair on his face. Some of the Indians of Tom's acquaintance have tattooed themselves, generally on the breast, with designs referring to their hunting experiences, or to crest privileges—a quarter-moon or a sea lion or a pair of Thunder-birds—but Tom has never bothered to do this. Aside from the head-flattening of infancy, Tom has never had any portion of his body mutilated, unless the perforation of his ears and the septum of his nose, for the attachment of ear and nose pendants of the bright rainbow-like abalone, strung by sinew threads, be considered a mutilation. These pendants, which he and other Indians have long discarded, were worn purely for ornament; they had no importance as ceremonial insignia. In spite of the fact that neither razor nor tweezers have ever smoothed out the hairy surface of his face, Tom has not altogether neglected the care of his body. To prevent chapping, he has often rubbed himself with tallow and red paint, and in his younger days he was in the habit of keeping himself in good condition by a cold plunge, at daybreak, in river or sea. The vigorous rubbing down with hemlock branches which followed, until the skin all tingled red, helped to give tone to his body. He could not afford to miss the plunge and rub-down for more than two or three days at a time, if only because to have done so would have brought upon him the contempt and derision of his comrades. No aspiring young hunter of the seal and the sea lion could allow himself to be called a woman. In the course of his long life Tom has painted his face in a great variety of ways, whether for festive occasions, or in the private quest of supernatural power in some secluded spot in the woods. Some of these face paints—and there are hundreds of them in use among the Nootka—are geometrical patterns, others are emblematic of supernatural beings and animals. Many of them, like the songs and dances with which they are associated, are looked upon as valuable privileges. It is long since Tom has worn or seen worn native costume—what little there was of it—but he distinctly remembers the blankets and cedar-bark garments that his people wore when he was a boy and, indeed, well on into his days of manhood. The heavy rains of the Coast, and the constant necessity of splashing in and out of the canoes along the beach, made tight-fitting garments and cumbrous foot- and leg-wear undesirable. The Nootka Indians wore no clinging shirts or leggings or moccasins. They are a barefoot and a barelegged people. Those of the men who could afford more than a breechclout wore a blanket robe loosely thrown about the body, either a hide—of bear or the far more valuable sea otter—or a woven blanket, whether of the inner-bark strands of the "yellow cedar" or the long, fleecy hair of the native dogs. The women wore cedar-bark "petticoats," which are nothing but loosely fitting girdles, fringed with long tassels of cedar bark. In rainy weather, they also wore woven hats of cedar-bark strands or split root fibers, round topped and cone-like. When the weather was thick and heavy with rain—and this happens often enough in the winter—both men and women wore raincapes of cedar bark or rush matting. The children ran about completely naked.

The food that Tom was accustomed to in his early days did not differ materially from his present fare. It was then, and is now, chiefly fish—boiled, steam-baked, spit-roasted, or smoked. In all his early haunts, in the houses and along the beach, everywhere he was immersed in grateful, fishy odors. From the earliest time that he can remember anything at all, he has been daily confronted by some aspect of the life of a fishing people, whether it be the catching of salmon trout by the boys with their two-barbed fish spears; or the spearing or trolling or netting of salmon by the older men; or the getting in the sea of herrings with herring rakes, of halibut with the peculiar, gracefully bent halibut hooks that every Indian even now has kicking around in his box of odds and ends, of cod with twirling decoys and spears that have two prongs of unequal length—"older" and "younger"; or the hanging up of salmon in rows to dry in the smoke houses, so that this all-important fish may still contribute his share of the food supply, long after the last salmon of the late fall has ceased to run; or the splitting up of the salmon by the women as a first preliminary to cooking; or any one of the hundreds of other scenes that make of a fisher folk a fish-handling and a fish-eating people. Second in importance to fish are the various varieties of edible shellfish and other soft bodied inhabitants of the sea—mussels and clams and sea urchins, sea cucumbers, and octopuses. The flesh of the octopus or "devil-fish," though not an important article of food, was considered quite a dainty, and feasts were often given in which it figured as a special feature, like crab apples or like the apples or oranges of present-day feasts. Far more important than these mushy foods, though probably subsidiary, on the whole, to salmon and other fish, was the flesh of sea mammals—the humpbacked whale, the California whale, the sea otter, the sea lion, and, most important of all, the hair seal.

Tom has harpooned his fill of seals in the course of his life and, like most other Nootka men of the last generation, has done a considerable amount of commercial sealing for white firms in Behring Sea. He has caught a few sea otters, which are now all but extinct, but no sea lions or whales, though he claims to have the hereditary privilege to hunt these animals, and to possess the indispensable magical knowledge without which their quest is believed by the Nootka to be doomed to failure.

Boiled whale and seal meat were highly prized and there was no more joyous event to break the monotony of tribal life than the towing to shore of a harpooned whale, or the drifting to shore of a whale carcass. In either case the flensing knives were quickly got ready, the carcass cut up, and feasts held in the village. Tom remembers how excitedly—he was then but a boy of ten or so—he once reported the appearance of a drifting whale carcass a quarter-mile from shore, how the whole village rushed into its canoes, and how they laboriously floated it on to the sandy beach, with their stout lanyards of cedar rope wound with nettle-fiber. The whale was cut up carefully, under the direction of a "measurer" into its traditionally determined portions, which were then distributed, according to hereditary right, to those entitled to receive them. Tom himself got the meat about the navel as a reward for his find. There was an unusual amount of whale oil tried out that time, and the fires at the feasts leaped higher than ever as the oil was thrown upon them, lighting up in lurid flashes the house posts carved into the likenesses of legendary ancestors.

Tom ate very little meat of land animals in his early days. Indeed, like most of the Coast people, he had a prejudice against deer meat and it was not until, as a middle-aged man, he had come into contact with some of the deer-hunting tribes of the interior of the island, that he learned to

prize it, though even to this day venison has not for him the toothsome appeal of a chunk of whale meat. Fish and meat were the staples, yet not the only foods. The women dug up a variety of edible roots such as clover and fern root, which made a welcome change, while blackberries, salmon berries, soapberries, and other varieties, frequently dried and pressed for winter consumption, added a sweetening to the somewhat monotonous fare. One relish Tom has never learned to enjoy—salt. All the older Nootka Indians detest salt in their food.

As Tom grew up, he became initiated into the chief handicrafts of his tribe. He got to be rather skillful at working in wood, both the soft red cedar and the hard yew and spiraea, familiarizing himself with the various wood-working processes—felling trees with wedges and stone hammers, splitting out planks, smoothing with adzes, drilling, handling the curved knife, steaming, and bending by the "kerfing" or notching process. Even in his youngest years, iron-bladed and iron-pointed tools had almost completely replaced the aboriginal implements of stone and shell, but the forms themselves, of the manufactured objects, underwent little or no modification down to the present day. In the course of his long life Tom has made hundreds of wooden articles of use—boxes with telescoping lids, paddles, bailers, fish clubbers, adze handles, ladles, bows, arrow shafts, fire drills, latrines, root diggers, fish spears, and shafts for sealing and whaling harpoons. He has also assisted in making dugout canoes, and has often prepared and put in position the heavy posts and beams of the large quadrangular houses that were still being built in his youth. On the other hand, Tom has never developed much aptitude in the artistic decoration of objects. Such things as paintings on house boards and paddles, or realistic carvings in masks, rattles, ornamental fish clubbers and house posts, are rather beyond his power and have had to be made for him, when required, by others more clever than himself. The one thing that Tom grew to be most proficient in was the preparation of house planks of desired lengths and widths. When he was a young man, he would travel about in canoes from village to village with the stock of planks he had on hand, and trade them for blankets, strings of dentalium shells, dried fish, whale oil, and other exchangeable commodities. It was through trading, rather than through personal success in fishing or hunting, that Tom amassed in time a considerable share of wealth, and it was through his wealth and the opportunity it gave him to make lavish distributions at potlatches or feasts, rather than through nobility of blood, that he came to occupy his present honorable position among his tribesmen.

While Tom and the other men, when they were not busy "potlatching" or visiting some relative, or taking a run down to Victoria, were engaged in fishing and sea mammal hunting and wood-working, the women prepared the food, dug for edible roots, gathered clams, and spent what time they could spare from these and similar tasks in the weaving and plaiting of blankets, matting, and baskets. What receptacles were not of wood were of basketry, while mats of various sorts did duty for tables, hangings, and carpeting. The materials of these baskets and mats, the omnipresent cedar bark and the rush, frayed easily, so that the women were kept constantly busy replenishing the household stock. Even now one can hardly enter a Nootka house without seeing one or more of the women twilling mats and baskets with strips of softened cedar bark or twining the cedar-bark strands into cordage and bags, or threading a rush mat with the long needles of polished spiraea. In the old days, there was always in the house a great clatter of breaking up the raw, yellow cedar bark with the corrugated bark beaters of bone of whale, and of loosening up the hard strips of red cedar bark into fibrous masses with the half-moon shredders. The women could work up the bark into almost any degree of fineness; indeed, the cedar-bark "wool" that was used to pad the cradles is almost as soft and fluffy in feel as down or cotton batting. When Tom was a boy, the women made only plain, unornamented baskets, whether twined or twilled, and ornamented the mats with sober, but effective lines of alder-dyed red and mud-dyed black. Since then, however, they have taken to making also trinket baskets and plaques of the peculiar wrapped weave, beautifully ornamented with realistic and geometrical designs in the black and white weft of grass. This art came to Tom's people from the Nitinats or Southern Nootka, who in turn owe it to the Makah of Cape Flattery. Trade with the whites is the chief incentive in the making of these finer specimens of basketry.

Nowadays the Nootka live in small frame houses, a family, in our narrower sense of the word, to a house. It was not so when Tom was young. The village of Hikwis, in which he was raised, consisted of a row of long plank houses, each constructed on a heavy quadrangular frame of posts, which were the trimmed trunks of cedars, and of crossbeams of circular section resting on the posts.

The roofing and walls were of cedar planks, running lengthwise of the house. The floor was the bare earth, stamped smooth, and a slightly raised platform ran along the rear and the long sides of the house. On the inner floor one or more fires were built, the smoke escaping through openings in the roof, provided by merely shoving a roofing plank or two to a side. Tom early learned not to stand erect in the house any more

than he could help. The smoke circulating in the upper reaches of the house, particularly in rainy weather when the smoke-hole rafters were closed, was trying to the eyes, and people found it convenient to sit or crouch on the floor as much as possible. Some of the houses, like the one in which Tom was brought up, had paintings or carvings referring to the crests or legendary escutcheons of the chief of the tribe, tribal subdivision, or house group. In Tom's house the main escutcheons were two Thunder-birds, face to face, painted on the outside of the wall planks; a series of round holes cut in the roof, and one in front that served as a door, all representing moons; and paintings of wolves on the boards that ran below the platforms. The chief of the house group, together with his immediate family, occupied the rear of the house; other families of lesser rank, kin to the chief by junior lines of descent, occupied various positions along the sides. Slaves were also housed in the long communal dwelling. They were not, like the middle class, undistinguished relations of the chief's families, but strangers, captured in war or bartered off like any chattels. The mat beds of the individual families were made on the platforms and were screened off from one another as required.

In such a house Tom early learned his exact relationship to all his kinsmen. He soon learned also the degree of his relationship to the neighboring house groups. He applied the terms "brother" and "sister" not only to his immediate brothers and sisters but to his cousins, near and remote, of the same generation. He distinguished, among all these remoter brothers and sisters, "older" and "younger," not according to their actual ages in relation to his own, but according to whether they belonged to lines of descent that were senior or junior to his own. Primogeniture, he gradually learned, both of self and progenitor, meant superiority in rank and privilege. Hence the terms "older" and "younger," almost from the beginning, took on a powerful secondary tinge of "superior" and "inferior." The absurdity of calling some little girl cousin, perhaps ten years his junior, his "older sister" was for him immensely less evident because of his ever present consciousness of her higher rank. As Tom grew older, he became cognizant of an astonishing number of uncles and aunts, grandfathers and grandmothers, of endless brothers-in-law—far and near. He was very much at home in the world. Wherever he turned, he could say, "Younger brother, come here!" or "Grandfather, let me have this." The personal names of most of his acquaintances were hardly more than tags for calling out at a distance, or at ceremonial gatherings.

Along with his feeling of personal relationship to individuals there grew up in Tom a consciousness of the existence of tribal subdivisions in the village. The Ts'isha'ath tribe, with which he was identified by residence, kinship, and upbringing, proved really to be a cluster of various smaller tribal units, of which the Ts'isha'ath, that gave their name to the whole, were the leading group. The other subdivisions were originally independent tribes that had lost their isolated distinctness through conquest, weakening in numbers, or friendly removal and union. Each of the tribal subdivisions or "septs" had its own stock of legends, its distinctive privileges, its own houses in the village, its old village sites and distinctive fishing and hunting waters that were still remembered in detail by its members. While the septs now lived together as a single tribe, the basis of the sept division was really a traditional local one. The sept grouping was perhaps most markedly brought to light at ceremonial gatherings. Tom learned in time that of all the honored seats recognized at a feast, a certain number of contiguous seats in the rear of the house belonged to representatives of the Ts'isha'ath sept, a certain number of others at the right corner in the rear to those of another sept, and so on. Thus, the proper ranking of the septs was ever kept before the eye by the definite assignment of seats of higher and lower rank.

But it must not be supposed that Tom's childhood and youth were spent entirely in work and in the acquirement of social and ceremonial knowledge. On the contrary, what interested him at least as much as sociology was play. He spun his tops—rather clumsy looking, two-pegged tops they were—threw his gaming spears in the spear and grass game and in the hoop-rolling game, hit feathered billets with a flat bat, threw beaver teeth dice (though this was chiefly a woman's game), and, when he grew older, took part in the favorite game of "lehal," the almost universal Western American guessing game, played with two or four gambling bones to the accompaniment of stirring songs. More properly belonging to the domain of sport was the somewhat dangerous game of canoe upsetting, in which the contestants upset their canoes and quickly righted them at a hand-clap signal. This was an especially favored game of Tom's. All through his life, up to the time that he lost his sight, he was as instinctively familiar with the run of water, the dip and lurch of

a canoe, and the turn of a paddle, as with the movements of walking on the land. Indeed, for days on end, at certain seasons, his life flowed on insistently to the very rhythm of rising and falling wave.

In at least one class of activities and beliefs Tom constantly received definite instruction from his father and maternal uncle. This was the world of unseen things, the mysterious domain of magic, of supernaturally compelling act and of preventive tabu. There were hundreds of things he must be careful to do or to avoid if he would have success in hunting and fishing, if he would be certain that unseen but ever present powers favor him in his pursuits or, at the least, desist from visiting harm upon him. He must be particularly careful not to anger the supernatural powers, among whom are to be counted the fish and mammals of the sea, by contamination with unclean things—and most obnoxious of all unclean things is the presence or influence of a menstruating or pregnant woman. For instance, a sealer or hunter of sea lions must not drag his canoe down to the water's edge, but have it carried over, as otherwise it might run over offal or some spot through which a menstruating woman had passed, and thus carry with it a scent that would frighten away the game. And one must be careful about his speech when hunting on the sea. A curious example of this is the fiction by which fur seal hunting is spoken of as gathering driftwood, the fur seal himself being referred to as "the one that sits yonder under a tree." It would not do to let him know too precisely what is going on while he is being hunted! The various tabus that Tom has learnt and practised in the course of his life are almost without number, and his practical success and longevity he ascribes in no small measure to his religious observance of them all.

The tabus are largely preventive measures. But Tom learned that there are more positive ways of working one's will in the world of magic. One of these is the use of certain amulets on the person, hidden in the house or woods, or in connection with hunting and fishing implements. As a general good-luck amulet, Tom was fond of wearing in his hat the spine of the "rat-fish." When his father was about to die, he called Tom to him and whispered in his ear an important secret. This was that the chief life-guarding amulet of the family had been a fire drill that was secreted at the bottom of an old box filled with all sorts of odds and ends. Its efficacy depended largely on the fact that hardly anybody knew of it. In general, secrecy helps tremendously in the power of all magic objects and formulae. An Indian likes to withhold as much as possible, even from his nearest kin, until economic urgency or the approach of death compels him to transmit the magical knowledge to some one that is near and dear to him. Some of his most powerful amulets Tom would secrete in the canoe or hide under the cherry bark wrappings around the hafts of his hunting spears. These amulets were of all sorts, but chiefly fragments of supernatural animals—blind snakes, crabs, spiders, or the like—obtained in the woods.

Some men are fortunate in getting power for hunting, fishing, wealth, love, doctoring, witchcraft, or whatever it may be, from supernatural beings or visitations. Amulets are often obtained in connection with these experiences, which regularly take place in mysterious or out-of-the-way places—the open sea, a remote island, the summit of a mountain, the heart of the woods—and of all mysteries, it is the mystery of the dark woods that most fascinates and inspires with dread the coast villager, so much at home on the sandy beach and on open sea spaces. The supernatural givers of power are a variegated and grotesque lot—mysterious hands pointing up out of the earth; the scaly, knife-tongued, lightning serpent; fairy-like beings; treacherous tree nymphs; hobgoblins; ogres; and strange hybrid animals that seem to have stepped out of nightmares. All these denizens of the supernatural world have power to bestow that may not with impunity be refused. This power, once obtained, must be carefully husbanded by the observance of requisite tabus.

Tom has not had as many supernatural experiences as some men, but he has nevertheless been favored by two or three striking visitations. A gnome-like being of the beneficent, wealth-giving class known as Chimimis, once appeared to him as he was sitting out at dusk in company with two other men. Though these companions had their eyes directed at the Chimimis, they could not perceive him. Tom alone, speechless with astonishment, saw him place two spears on the roof of the house, walk off to the neighboring house, and disappear, so it seemed, in a log. When Tom came to himself, he scraped off those parts of the spear shafts that the hand of the Chimimis had gripped. He preserved the scrapings as an amulet and, in time, became one of the wealthiest men of his tribe.

At another time Tom obtained power from a supernatural being known as "Full-eyed," a diminutive, brownie-like creature. He was lying

very ill in the house, gazing steadfastly at the fire, when the popping up of a little cinder caused him to raise his eyes. He saw what seemed to be a child circling the fire in a counter-clockwise direction, which is the exact opposite of the Nootka direction in dancing. He knew immediately that it was Full-eyed. The brownie carried a small storage basket on his breast, and picked up from the floor anything he could lay his hands on. Though Tom had been unable to sit up straight, this supernatural experience infused him with such sudden strength that he was now easily able to sit up.

He believed also that, from this time on, wealth rolled into his house more rapidly than ever. The third of Tom's supernatural experiences was less striking than the other two, but apparently equally potent in its practical results. Tom was reclining on the sleeping platform of the house, in the dead of winter, when he observed a strange thing in one of the storage baskets on the box that marked the head of his bed. He noticed that a big black bumblebee gave birth to an infant bee. This seemed remarkable and evidently significant in view of the fact that the young bees ordinarily come into being in the summer, only. Because Tom was sole witness to so strange an occurrence, he was more than ever favored in the accumulation of wealth.

Such extraordinary occurrences as these are clearly in the nature of accidents; they cannot be relied upon for the necessary aid in the successful prosecution of life's work. The standard, and on the whole, the most useful means of securing this necessary aid is by the performance of secret rituals. Nothing came to one who did not undergo considerable hardship in training. This Tom learned early in life. If he wished to be a successful fisherman, or a hunter of sea mammals, or a land hunter, he had to retire at certain seasons to secret places in the woods, known only to the respective families that frequented them. Here, for days on end, he would bathe, rub himself down with hemlock branches until the skin tingled with pain, pray to the Sky Chief for long life and success, and, most important of all, carry out secret, magical performances based on the principle of imitation. If he wished to obtain power in sealing, he would build effigies of twigs representing the seal, the harpooning outfit, and the hunting canoe. The aspirants for success would dramatize the future hunt in its magical setting. He himself performed imitative actions and offered continuous prayers for success. These periods of preparation tested physical endurance to the utmost; fasting, continuous wakefulness, sexual continence, and the observance of all sorts of tabus formed part of the training. There was little that one could not learn to do, if only he were hardy enough to undergo the necessary magical preparation. Such young men as were fired with extraordinary ambitions, say unusual success in whaling or the acquirement of potent shamanistic power, would train the will and chasten the cries of the flesh for incredibly long periods, their spiritual eye fixed singly on the austerities of magical procedure.

Tom never devoted himself to unusual rigors in the acquirement of magical power. He contented himself with the normal routine enjoined upon those planning to seal, to spear salmon, to troll, to catch halibut with hooks, to spear cod with the aid of decoys, to accumulate wealth, to prepare for ritualistic performances, and to obtain enough shamanistic power to withstand the attempts of evil-minded people to bewitch him. He never ventured upon the more difficult and exhausting procedures required to make a successful whaler or hunter of sea lions. Of the more unusual types of secret ritual, Tom attempted but one. When past middle-age, he was fired with the ambition to learn how to interpret the speech of ravens. The ravens are believed to be the supernatural messengers of the wolves, the most austere and eerie of all beings, in the belief of the Nootka. Could Tom have learned to unravel the mysteries concealed in the croakings of these supernatural birds, there is little doubt that he would have been able to advance in ritual power far beyond his fellow tribesmen. Unfortunately he found the quest of this difficult knowledge too exhausting, too baffling. Tom acknowledges his failure with a sigh.

The secret rituals could only be performed at auspicious periods, when the moon was waxing and when the days were becoming progressively long. It was for this reason that Tom was always very careful to keep track of the passage of time, of the recurrence of the moons. If some neighbor, less wise and observant, committed the error of taking one moon for another and of performing magical rituals out of season, Tom would say nothing. He would smile and keep counsel with himself, knowing well that his neighbor's efforts when the hunting season came around, were doomed to failure. While Tom was one of those that never went out of his way to bewitch his neighbors or to spoil their luck, he was naturally not altogether displeased when they put themselves at a disadvantage. It was none of his business to correct them, to strengthen the hands of possible rivals.

Medicine men gained their power in a manner perfectly analogous to all other quests for magical assistance. The difference was simply that they sought aid of such beings as were known to grant power to cure diseases and to counteract witchcraft. The material guardians and amulets obtained by medicine men, generally certain birds and rarer fish, were locked away in their breasts. When required for the detection of sickness, for the cure of the diseased, or for the overcoming of an evil opponent, they could be called upon to fly invisibly to the desired goal and to return at will. Tom himself obtained a modicum of power from the mallard ducks, but not enough to warrant his considering himself a regular practitioner. He had, also, a certain inherited, shamanistic power, or rather privilege, that came to him from a Nitinat ancestor. This is why at public shamanistic performances which form part of the Ts'ayek cult, Tom's oldest son has the right to initiate shamanistic novices at a certain point in the ceremonial procedure, though he himself is not a practising medicine man.

Many Nootka are accused of gaining power to bewitch their enemies or rivals, whether by the handling of their food, nail parings, and body effluvia, or by the pronouncing of direful spells in connection with the name and effigy of the hated person. Tom never indulged in such mean spirited pursuits, but he is very sure that many of his acquaintances have done so. It is the constant fear of witchcraft that even to this day causes the Indians to keep many dogs around the house, and to lock their doors securely at night. The barking of the dogs is useful in calling attention to malevolent "pains" or minute disease objects that wander about, particularly at night, while the locking of doors is essential in denying these objects an entrance.

The great supernatural beings of Nootka belief, such as the Sky-Chief, the Thunder-bird, and the Wolves, loomed very large in Tom's life, whether in prayer or in ritual. Certain Nootka are more deeply religious than others. They are more fervent in their prayers and they work themselves up to a greater ecstasy in the performance of rituals that are sacred to divine powers. In contrast to men of this type, Tom has always been rather sober, not a skeptic by any means, but not an emotional enthusiast. His knowledge of religious ceremonials is vast,

but the spirit that animates this knowledge is rather one of order, of legal particularity, not of spiritual ecstasy. The practical economical world, the pursuit of gain, has always been more congenial to Tom's temperament. This does not mean that Tom is a rationalist in matters relating to the unseen world. Only the educated or half-educated half-breeds are rationalists, and more than one of them has angered Tom by his ill-advised attempts to disturb him with skeptical arguments. However, there has been no change in Tom. He knows, as firmly as he knows his own name, that when the rumble of thunder is heard from the mountain, it is because the Thunder-bird is leaving his house on the peak, flapping his wings heavily, as he makes off for the sea to prey upon the whales. He knows also that when those that are not blind like himself tell him that there has been a flash of lightning, it is because the Thunder-bird has dropped the belt wound about his middle. This belt is the lightning serpent, zig-zagging down to the earth or coiling in a flash around a cedar tree.

Aside from the elementary problem of making his living, a Nootka's main concern is to earn the esteem of his fellow tribesmen by a lavish display of wealth. It is not enough for him to accumulate it and to live in private ease. He must, from time to time, invite the other families of his tribe, and the neighboring tribes, to public ceremonies known as potlatches, in which one or more of the important privileges to which he is entitled are shown and glorified by the distribution of property to the guests. The exhibiting of privileges may take several forms. The most important of them refer to ancestral crests, which may be shown in a dramatic performance, as a picture on a board, or latterly, on canvas, or symbolized in a dance. Ceremonial games are another frequent type of exhibitions of privileges at certain potlatches. Nearly all privileges have their proper songs, which are themselves jealously guarded privileges, and which are sung on these occasions.

There are two considerations that make the public performance of the more important privileges a matter of the greatest moment. In the first place, a man must clearly indicate his right to its performance by recounting the origin myth that it dramatizes, and by tracing his personal connection with the originator of the privilege. In the second place, he must be careful to distribute at least as much property as has already been distributed in his family, in connection with the public presentation of the privilege. If it is at all possible, he will try to exceed the record, so as to add to the public prestige not only of himself and his immediate family, but of the privilege itself. Should he fail in either of these essential respects, he is shamed. Hence, an important potlatch is not to be lightly undertaken. It requires much careful thought and preparation, and it necessitates the gathering of enough wealth to pay for all the services rendered by singers and other assistants, to present substantial gifts to the guests, and to feed the crowd of men, women and children that are present at the ceremony.

A potlatch is not often given as a mere display of wealth. Nearly always it is combined with some definite social or religious function, such as the giving of a name, the coming to marriageable age of a daughter, marriage, a mourning ceremony, the Wolf ritual, or a doctoring ceremony. Potlatching in its fundamental sense, in other words the giving away of property to the guests, is an essential of practically all ceremonies, big or little, religious or profane. Every potlatch involves at least three parties, the giver, the guest or guests, and the person in whose honor the potlatch is given. The last of these is generally some young member of the family whose prestige is thus furthered early in life, but it may be a stranger who has done the giver a service. There are different kinds of gifts. Certain of them are ceremonial grants to which the highest in rank of the tribe are entitled, but which they are expected to return with one hundred per cent interest at a subsequent potlatch. Another class of gifts, which feature the most important and picturesque part of the potlatch, is made to the highest in rank among the guests. There is no rigid rule as to the return of these gifts, but in practice they are nearly always liquidated at a return potlatch, with gifts of an equal, and in many cases greater, value. Finally, towards the end of the potlatch, there is a general distribution of smaller amounts to the crowd. Less careful account is taken of the return of such gifts than of the first two types. In part, the giving of a potlatch amounts to an investment of value, though it is doubtful whether, among the Nootka, the greater part of the expenditure incurred at a potlatch ever returned to its owner.

A potlatch serves not only a definite social and economic purpose for its giver, but affords, as well, an opportunity for minor distributions of property, such as public payments for services, on the part of other individuals present. Indeed any announcements of importance, such as the handing over of a privilege or a change in name, would be most appropriately made at a potlatch. The assembled tribesmen and guests were, to all intents and purposes, witnesses to such announcements.

Tom began to give potlatches on his own account when still quite a young man. The first one of any importance that he was responsible for, was a potlatch in honor of his niece's husband. This was a man of low birth, whom Tom had vowed to have nothing to do with. When his niece, however, gave birth to a child, Tom relented and, in order to wash away the stain on his family's honor, he called together thirty of his relatives, and distributed four guns and a blanket to each. He also sang two of his privileged songs, which he then and there transferred to the child as its due privilege. This potlatch not only marked a reconcilement with his low-born nephew, but gave the little youngster a fair start in life in the race for status. The next of Tom's potlatches was a Wolf ritual, in which he himself performed two of the ceremonial dances, those of the Thunder-bird and the Wolf circling about on all fours.

Some time after this, Tom resolved to marry a Ts'isha'ath girl named Witsah. In spite of the fact that she was a member of his own tribe, Tom wooed the girl not as a Ts'isha'ath, but as a member of a Nitinat tribe, among whom he had kinsmen on his father's side. As his own father was dead, he had ten of his Nitinat uncles woo the girl on his behalf. The wooing is always an important part of the marriage preliminaries, and consists chiefly in the placing of objects, symbolizing one or more of the privileges of the suitor, outside the house of the girl's family. The suitor himself is not present. Sometimes the objects are refused, when the suit may be continued until an acceptance is gained, though this does not necessarily follow. The suitor privileges deposited by Tom's representatives consisted of ten fires and a carving, representing the lightning serpent. These were accepted and returned to Tom's uncle as an indication of willingness on the part of the bride's parents to proceed with the marriage ceremony. Not long after the return of the privileges, the marriage ceremony was celebrated among the Ts'isha'ath people. The money distributed at that time by Tom and his Nitinat relatives constituted a bridal purchase, but when Tom's first child was born, the property then distributed was returned to Tom and the Nitinats with interest.

The greater part of the marriage ceremony consists of the performance of ceremonial games, each of which is accompanied by special songs, and followed by distributions of property. These games symbolize the difficulty of obtaining the hand of the bride, referring as they do to legendary tests that suitors were compelled to undergo in the past, before they could be admitted by the bride's father. One of the tests, for instance, might be the lifting of an especially heavy stone, or standing for some time without flinching between two fires. According to legendary theory such tests should be endured by the bridegroom himself, but in actual ceremonial practice any one of the bridegroom's party may be the winner in the contest, and receive the prize from the bride's father or whoever of her people is the proud possessor of that particular marriage-game privilege.

Some time after his marriage Tom gave two potlatches in a single month. The first of these was a puberty potlatch in behalf of a younger sister of his. The second was a birth feast or, as the Nootka term it a "navel feast" for his first child, a boy. About a year later Tom invited the Ucluelet people, one of the Nootka tribes, to a feast at which many dance privileges were performed and much property distributed. By this time Tom was getting to be pretty well known among the tribes of the west coast of Vancouver Island, for his rapidly growing wealth and for his potlatches. It was, therefore, no surprise to him, though it proved very gratifying, to have the chief of the Ahousat, one of the most powerful of the northern Nootka tribes, especially invite him to a potlatch at which he was given four of the chief's ceremonial songs. In return, Tom gave a potlatch to the Ahousat and the Comox, a tribe of alien speech from the east coast of the Island. He distributed four hundred blankets to the former, three hundred to the latter.

A year or two after this potlatch, occurred the decisive event in Tom's social career. This was the birth of his first daughter. The most magnificent Nootka potlatches are generally given in connection with a daughter's puberty ceremony. Ever since his marriage, Tom had been hoping to be able, in the fullness of time, to make a record in potlatching among his people, and to show his most valued privileges at the puberty potlatch of a daughter. Now that he was actually blessed by the arrival of a little girl, Tom's plans took immediate shape. He set about the accumulation of property with more zest than ever, driving many a sharp bargain with the Indians and whites, and he revolved frequently in his mind what tribes he was to invite, and what dramatic displays, dances and songs he was to use at the great ceremony. His first concern was to build a large house of native construction that the guests were to enter when invited to the Ts'isha'ath people. Appropriate timbers for posts and beams are not easy to find, especially since the white man's sawmill has made its appearance in the country. Hence, Tom was indefatigable in making inquiries of various persons and keeping his eye out for sufficiently large and conveniently located cedars. As he found such trees, he had them felled, hauled up to the Ts'isha'ath village along the Somass river, and put in place as opportunity presented itself. The actual construction of the house was thus spread over a period of some ten or fifteen years.

At one time an unfortunate casualty occurred. One of the heavy crossbeams fell to the ground, fortunately without injuring any one, but the event was considered an ill omen. Nevertheless, Tom did the best he could to ward off the evil influence by having a dance performed in honor of the spirit of the beam. Special songs that he possessed for this purpose were sung at the time.

Tom hoped that he could have the house completed before his daughter arrived at maturity. He was doomed to disappointment. His house still lacked one of the crossbeams and all the lighter woodwork, when his wife announced to him one morning that their daughter had come of age, was menstruating, in other words, for the first time. There was nothing for it but to have the puberty ceremony performed at once, reserving the main puberty potlatch for a few months later. Tom painted his face red and invited the neighboring Hopach'as'ath tribe to the puberty ceremony, the "torches standing on the ground," as it is termed.

This ceremony marks the beginning of the period of seclusion of the girl. She is painted and ornamented for the occasion, generally with legendary insignia belonging to the family, is made to stand in front of two long boards painted with representations of Thunder-birds and whales, and has water thrown four times at her feet. Four or ten poles, the so-called "torches," are lighted and later distributed with gifts to those entitled to receive them. Songs of various types are sung, particularly satirical songs twitting the opposite sex. Ceremonial games, some of them anticipating later marriage games, are also performed and prizes are distributed. After a general distribution of goods, the guests depart, leaving the girl to fast for four days and to enter upon a secluded period of various tabus behind the painted boards in the rear of the house.

After the puberty ceremony, Tom proceeded to Victoria to lay in his store of supplies for the impending potlatch. He bought an enormous number of boxes of biscuits, and to this day nothing pleases him more than to tell of how he compelled the white merchant to give him a special rate on the unusual order. As soon as the provisions were safely deposited at his village, Tom invited twelve tribes to his potlatch. To the nearer tribes he sent messengers; the more remote tribes of the east coast he invited in person. When the appointed day arrived, the Ts'isha'ath found that they had on their hands by far the largest number of guests that had ever visited the tribe at a single time. It was the proudest moment of Tom's life. Everything went well. There was enough food for all, the distributions of property were generous, and all the privileges were interestingly presented. There were a considerable number of these privileges performed, one or two of them being fairly elaborate dramatic representations that were new even to the most northern Nootka tribes, great potlatchers though they are. Tom's hereditary claim to the performances, the dances and the songs, was carefully explained by the ceremonial speaker. The ancestral legends were in every case recounted at length. Tom's title to the special crests of the whale and the Thunder-bird was duly set forth. The explanation of the carved house posts took the speaker back to the creation of the first Ts'isha'ath man from the thigh of a woman. Due account, as usual in these origin legends, was taken of the flood. The potlatch securely established Tom's position among the Indians of the Island. To this day it is often referred to by the Ts'isha'ath and their neighbors. Tom's family was "put high" as never before. More than once, Tom's grandson has found himself, when visiting comparative strangers, say among the East Coast tribes, received with open arms and honored with gifts of great value, all on the strength of his grandfather's potlatch.

Tom's potlatching career did not end here. Some time later he invited the Kyuquot, a Nootka tribe adjoining the Kwakiutl. At this potlatch he gave a dramatic representation of a number of privileges, including two Thunder-birds, a spouting whale, the supernatural quartz-beings known as He'na, and a supernatural bird known as Mihtach, a sort of mallard duck that haunts the top of the mountain called "Two-bladders-on-its-summit." The Heshkwiat tribe of Nootka was the next to be invited to a potlatch. A year or two after this, the second greatest ceremonial event in Tom's career took place, in the form of his second Wolf ritual or Tlokwana. The ritual was given for the special benefit of his oldest son Douglas and his newly married wife. These were the chief initiates in the ritual. Curiously enough, Tom's little grandson, as yet unborn, was also initiated. This is an extreme instance of the tendency of the Nootka Indians to heap honors upon their offspring at the earliest possible opportunity.

The Wolf ritual is the most awesome, the most fascinating and fear-inspiring ceremony that the Nootka possess. Whatever religious exaltation or frenzy they are capable of, finds expression in this elaborate ritual. The performance, which generally lasts eight days, preferably in the winter, is dominated throughout by the spirit of the wolves who are believed to be hovering near at the outskirts of the village. The more important parts of the ceremonial are open to only such members of the tribe as have been initiated. Many tabus must be observed by those participating, and an attitude of highminded seriousness must be maintained throughout. In the old days, frivolity during the more strictly religious parts of the ritual, aside of course from the ceremonial buffoonery, was very severely punished by the marshaling attendants. Spearing to death on the spot was the penalty for infraction of the most sacred tabus.

The ritual begins with the songs and other ceremonial activities of an ordinary potlatch. Rumors are set going of the appearance of wolves in the neighborhood of the village. These rumors, accentuated by tales of narrow escapes and bloody casualties, act powerfully upon the imagination of the children, who are soon reduced to a state of panic. All of a sudden the lights are extinguished, and the four "wolves" break through the side of the house. In the confusion that ensues they make off with the youngsters that are to be initiated.

From this moment, begins the ritual proper. A certain number of the tribe have the hereditary privilege to "play wolf," that is, to act as wolves during certain parts of the ritual beyond the confines of the village, to make off with the novices, and keep these as supposed prisoners in the woods. For a number of days, there are supposed to be unsuccessful attempts to take back the captured novices, but the wolves remain obdurate until certain songs are sung, when the novices are brought out in view of the people and the series of attacks finally succeeds in routing the wolves. The novices are supposed to be frenzied by the spirits of various

supernatural beings that possess them. They must be brought back by force. Those privileged to do so lasso them, and, to the accompaniment of sacred songs, the struggling novices are conducted to the potlatch house, whistling furiously all the while. The hubbub of mingled whistling, drumming and simultaneous singing of many distinct ritual songs, continues for the greater part of the night. The din is indescribable. During the following day is performed the most sacred episode in the ritual. The whistling spirits that possess the novices must be exorcised by means of sacred dances and songs. A purification ceremony of bathing in the river or sea follows. The remainder of the ritual consists of the performance of a number of special dances, each of which is appropriate to the particular supernatural being that is supposed to have possessed one of the initiates. There are many of these dances, varying greatly in their prestige as privileges, and in their character of religious frenzy. Probably the most austere of the dances is that of the supernatural wolf, who crawls about in reckless pursuit of destruction and has to be restrained with great difficulty by a number of attendants. Other dances represent various types of woodsy creatures or ogres. Many of them are pantomimic representations of animals, while human activities of various kinds are represented in still others.

With this Wolf ritual Tom's ceremonial activities gradually lessened. He continued to take an active interest in whatever potlatches were given by his family, and he often helped with his advice and active cooperation in the singing of songs and the delivering of ceremonial addresses, particularly of the formal speeches of thanks. Now that he had done his share in establishing the glory of his family, Tom sat back and allowed his eldest son to take the initiative, at least in theory, in all ceremonies affecting their standing in the tribe.

It is long since Tom has been able to do useful work. He is entirely dependent on his oldest son's family, with whom he lives, but they do not feel his presence to be a burden. For one thing, he is uniformly good-natured, very talkative about his own past and in judging his neighbors, and always ready to help with his advice in matters of importance, whether it be the preparations for a potlatch or some contested sealing claim. But back of the garrulous, shabby Tom of the present, looms up the Tom of the great potlatches of former days. It is to this Tom that his children and grandchildren almost entirely owe the high standing that they maintain among their people. When Tom dies he will be put in a coffin and buried in the ground. This was not the old Nootka custom. The more important families had caves in which their deceased members were put away; others were laid in burial boxes or rush mats which were then put up in trees back of the village. Near the place of the burial there would be put up a grave post, constructed of roof rafters of the house, on which would be painted one of the crests of the deceased.

Though the old burial customs are no longer followed, some of the beliefs and practices attending death have not yet died out. Thus, the immediate personal effects of the deceased, as well as considerable additional property, are always destroyed. In the old days the whole house might be burned down, and tales are told of how the mourning survivors would move off to another spot to build them a new house. In all likelihood there will be performed immediately after Tom's death a ceremony intended to comfort the family of the deceased and to induce Tom's spirit to leave the house and its vicinity. Tom's soul will have left his body in the shape of a tiny shadow-like double of himself, through the crown of his head, to assume eventually the form of a full-fledged ghost. It is safe to assume that the tabu of the dead person's name will be carefully observed. Not only will Tom's name not be mentioned by his tribesmen for a stated period, but all words that involve the main element of his name will be carefully avoided. This element denotes the idea of "distant." People will have to get along as best they can without it, whether by beating about the bush, by stretching the meaning of some other element so as to enable it to take its place, or, if need be, by borrowing the corresponding element, provided it be of different sound, from some other dialect. Wailing sounds will be heard in the village for some time after Tom's death, and it is very likely that at a mourning potlatch a number of privileges belonging to the family, say four songs, will be thrown away. Such privileges are tabued during the mourning period. At the end of the mourning period, which may be anything from a year to ten, another potlatch is given by one of the family and the tabus are lifted. When that time arrives Tom's name will have passed into native history. The name Sayach'apis, "Stands-up-high-over-all," will then be freely referred to with pride or with envy.

Edward Sapir

AN ESKIMO WINTER

The skin boat, propelled by the oars of the women, approached the shores. On the bundles of caribou skins which were piled up in the stern, steering cautiously through the floes of drift ice that dotted the surface of the sea, sat Pakkak, the boat-owner. The boat was heavily laden and a strong tide was running so that the women had to exert themselves, two on each oar, to make headway. Pakkak's son accompanied the boat in his kayak. He had been out seal hunting in order to keep the traveling party supplied with provisions. The seals lay on the narrow deck of his boat which zig-zagged swiftly through the water, propelled by the strokes of the single paddle which he held in the middle, and which struck the water, now at the right and now at the left.

The young man was the first to reach the shore. He brought his boat sideways close to the beach and climbed out of the small central hatch in which he had been sitting. He took off his harpoon and lance, his bird spear and float from under the holding thongs. Then he unlashed the seals, and hauled them ashore. After everything had been taken off, he lifted the light boat out of the water, turned it over, put his head into the opening and carried it up the shore.

Meanwhile, the whole party in the large boat had reached the land. It was nearly high water. The travelers jumped ashore. The children and old people scrambled out of the boat, and the tent covers, poles and household goods were taken ashore. The caribou skins, which were the spoils of the summer's hunt inland, were deposited on a dry spot. While the women climbed the barren hills to gather brush for building a fire, the men hauled up the boat, and put up the tent. The framework was quickly set up, the skin cover was thrown over it, and the lower part of the skin was ballasted with stones. When the women came back, the shrubs were put down in the rear of the tent. They were covered with

heavy caribou skins, and thus the bed of the family was prepared. The seals were put down at the right and left of the doorway, inside.

After a short time, the boats of Pakkak's brothers came in. They had started together in the morning, but had made unequal progress through the lanes of water that opened between the shifting ice floes. After unloading the boats, the brothers also put up their tents.

Some of the women had piled up the fuel nearby. Pakkak fanned into flames the smoldering slow match which he was carrying along. As soon as he had obtained fire, the shrubs were lighted. Meanwhile, the hunter had opened one of the seals and removed the skin with the attached blubber. He cut off pieces of the blubber and threw them into the flames. The rectangular kettle, hollowed out of a block of soft soapstone, was filled with water and placed over the fire. The seal meat was put into it, and soon the water began to boil. When the meat was done, the men and women had finished their work, and Pakkak stood next to the kettle and shouted, "Boiled meat, boiled meat!"

The men sat down in a circle near the fire. The women formed another circle. Pakkak took one piece of the meat out of the kettle, and handed it to one of the men; he gave another piece to one of the women. The first person bit into the meat and cut off a mouthful close to his lips. Then he passed the meat to his neighbor, who in the same way cut off a mouthful and passed the meat on. Thus, the whole company was provided for.

The travelers were tired from their exertions, and retired to their beds in the rear of the tent where the whole family lay down, their heads toward the door. They covered themselves with the large blanket of caribou skins which extended over the whole width of the bed from one side of the tent to the other.

Pakkak and his brothers, and Usuk, the half-witted old bachelor who lived with them, were the first to arrive at the place of the winter village, but within a few days other families came, who had been hunting in various districts. Men and women would sit together until late at night, telling of their summer experiences and of their success in hunting. Pakkak and his brothers had been hunting on the shores of the inland lake to which they used to resort, where they had fallen in with large herds of caribou. Some of the men drove the animals into the water, while others pursued them in their frail boats. The animals were easily overtaken and killed with the lance.

Pakkak was the oldest one of five brothers who were all skillful hunters, and provided well for their families. They were renowned for their daring and enterprise. Therefore, their friendship was valued and their enmity feared. Pakkak was held in particular awe, for he was not only strong in body and skilled in the use of the knife, lance and bow, but he was endowed with supernatural powers. As a child he had sat on the knees of the old medicine man, Shark, who had been known to visit the moon and the great deity that controls the supply of sea animals. Through contact with him, the supernatural power had passed into Pakkak's body, and now his services were needed whenever sickness and famine visited the village. Thus it happened, that Pakkak and his brothers were both sought as protectors and shunned as possessed of unusual power.

Pakkak did not misuse his power, but one of his brothers, Ikeraping, was rash in anger and overbearing in manner, and he was feared and hated. If it had not been for the combined strength of the brothers, the people of the winter village would have agreed to do away with Ikeraping in order to rid themselves of his aggressions.

Among the later arrivals was No-tongue, whose party had been unsuccessful in the summer hunt. He had hunted in the narrow valleys between the ice covered highlands, and by mischance he had come at a time when the caribou had left for another feeding ground. He had only a few skins for his whole family, hardly sufficient to provide himself, his old mother Petrel, his wife, Attina, and his children, with the necessary winter clothing. However, he was not greatly perturbed. He relied upon good luck and the help of his friends who might be expected to assist him, in case they should have skins to spare.

Gradually, one party after another arrived, and on the island which a short time ago had been solitary and quiet, little groups of huts sprang up and there was great activity. The women were busy with their household duties, getting fuel and mending clothes, while the men went out hunting in their kayaks and brought home game for their evening meal. The skins of the seals were scraped by the women, and stretched on the ground to be dried and later on worked into tent covers.

The wind had shifted seaward, and the floating ice had been driven away from the shore. It was getting cold, and the ponds began to be

covered with a thin sheet of ice. Before the sea began to freeze over, it was necessary to bring the dogs back from the islands on which they had been placed over summer, and where they lived on what they could find on the beach or what they could hunt on the hills. Only a few of them had been taken along on the summer hunt, and with them were brought back a few litters of pups that were carefully nursed by the women.

When the new ice began to form on the sea, the hunters could not go
out any more in their boats, because the sharp edges of the ice would have
cut the skin covers. For a few days, all were confined to the land. The
hunters brought in ptarmigans and hares, but everybody looked anxiously
forward to the time when the ice would be strong enough for the hunters
to go out. A few days without new supplies are likely to empty the larder
all too quickly. Besides, it was getting cold, and work on winter clothing
could not be started until the sea was covered with ice. The Sea-Goddess
would take bitter revenge if such a sin were committed.

This year the weather was favorable, and the anxious days between
summer and winter were not needlessly prolonged. After three cold
days, the men could go out on the sea ice and wait at the edge of the open
water for the seals to come up to breathe. Since the wind had brought
back the drifting ice, the stretch of open water was not very wide, and
the seals came near enough to be harpooned without difficulty, and to be
drawn up to the ice. It was even possible to venture out in the open water
in the kayak, for the ice was not forming very rapidly. Thus an ample
supply of meat was obtained.

Meanwhile, the women were busy scraping and cleaning the caribou
skins, and making the winter clothing for the family—the warm shirts
and drawers of young caribou skins, and the heavy jackets and trousers
of heavy skins; the stockings of light skins of young caribou, and the
boots made from the skin of caribou legs, with soles of ground sealskins.
Poor No-tongue had just enough for his family, and a few skins to spare.
Unfortunately the catch of the whole community had been rather light,
notwithstanding Pakkak's good luck.

From now on, the men went out regularly every morning and came
back in the evening, generally with an ample catch. One day they had
gone out again and were scattered along the edge of the ice, watching for
seals. During the day the sky clouded up, and a strong, seaward wind
began to blow. It increased in strength, and an ominous cracking of the
ice gave warning of danger. Hurriedly the men loaded their sledges, and
sped landward. Under their feet the ice began to crack and to yield to the
pressure of the wind, but they succeeded in reaching land before the floe
gave way and drifted out to sea.

Only No-tongue's sledge was missing. He had been hunting on a
projecting point of ice, and before he was even aware of his danger,

the whole point had broken off and was rapidly drifting out to sea.
There was nothing for him to do but yield to his fate, and see whether the gale would exhaust itself soon, and whether by chance the floe
that carried him might be blown back to land. Fortunately he had
just killed a seal. He flensed it and made a little shelter of the fresh
hide.

His lance had to serve as a tent pole. He protected his tent cover against the wind by piling snow all over it. He made a receptacle for the blubber out of a piece of skin, and thus improvised a little lamp. Fortunately, too, he carried his fire drill and a little of the moss which is used for wicks; so that he was able to start a little fire in his shelter. The gale was still blowing, and the angry waves threatened to break up the floe on which he was drifting. When day dawned the land was far away. Soon, however, the wind subsided, and a swift tide carried the ice floe back, nearer and nearer the land.

It had grown very cold. An icy slush was forming on the surface of the sea and the waves were rapidly calming down. The breaking up of the floe which seemed imminent through the night was no longer to be feared and immediate danger of drowning had passed. Still it was doubtful how the drift would end. With the changing tide, the current changed again, and the floe drifted away from the shore. The play of tides continued for days. Now the shore seemed near, so that the hopes of No-tongue were raised to a high pitch, and now the shore receded. In these days of anxiety No-tongue never lost courage, but, mocking his own misfortune, he composed this song:

> Aya, I am joyful; this is good!
> Aya, there is nothing but ice around me, that is good!
> Aya, I am joyful; this is good!
> My country is nothing but slush, that is good!
> Aya, I am joyful; this is good!
> Aya, when indeed, will this end? this is good!
> I am tired of watching and waking, this is good!

His endurance and patience were finally rewarded. After a week of privations, he reached the shore not very far from the winter village. A few days of hard travel over the ice covered sea, and rocky hills brought him home to his family and friends. They had almost given him up for lost.

As it grew colder the light tent no longer offered adequate protection. The women sewed a new cover of sealskins and gathered loads of brush. They placed them on the outside of the summer tent, and spread the new covers over the whole structure. The door flap was also transformed into a solid wall, and only a low opening was left, through which the people had to pass, stooping down low. This darkened the inside of the tent, which before had been fairly light because the front part of the tent cover was made of the transparent inner membrane of sealskin. Therefore the lamps were put into place. The long, rectangular entrance of the tent with its roof-shaped cover still served for keeping provisions, but just in front of the beds, the soapstone lamps—long crescent-shaped vessels—were placed. The wife of the tent owner took her seat on the bed in front of the lamp, where she sat in kneeling position letting her body rest between her heels. The lamp was filled with blubber that had been chewed to release the oil, and the straight front edge of the lamp was provided with a wick of moss which, when carefully treated with the bone pointer, gave an even, yellow flame that lighted and heated the hut pleasantly.

Soon the snow began to fall, and the autumnal gales packed it solid in every hollow in the ground, and piled it up against the sides of the huts. The heather-like shrubs were deeply buried under the snow, and all domestic work had to be done inside. The soapstone cooking vessels were placed over the lamps, and all the meals were prepared in the house. The entrance to the hut was protected against the cold by a low passage, built of snow. As it grew colder, the snow accumulated, and most of the people exchanged their tents for snow houses. The men cut out of an even snow bank blocks about thirty inches by eighteen inches high, and six inches wide. These they placed on edge, in the form of a circle. At one point, the upper edge of the row was cut down to the ground, and then sliced down to the right, so that it slanted up gradually. At the place where it had been cut down, a new block of snow was put on, leaning against the end of the first row and slightly inclined inward. One man was cutting the snow blocks outside, while his helper was placing the blocks from the inside—each block being inclined slightly more inward so that a spiral wall was gradually formed. Finally the key block was inserted, and the builder cut a little door through which he came out. In the rear half of the circular room, a platform was built for the bed which was elevated a couple of feet above the ground, and at the same level, at the right and left of the entrance, a bank was erected. The bed platform was covered with shrubs and skins. The tent cover was used to line the inside of the snow house, being held to the wall by means of pegs and ropes, thus protecting the snow against the heat of the living room. The lamps were put in place on each side of the front of the bed platform, and the pots were hung over them. In front, just above the door, a window was cut which was covered with a translucent sheet, made of seal intestines sewed together, and a series of low vaulted structures was erected in front of the door, forming a passageway which protected the inside against the wind. When everything was done the family moved into the snow house. Two families occupied one house and each housewife had her seat in front of her lamp. The stores of meat were placed on the platforms at the right and left. Now the regular winter life began. It was bitter cold. The dogs huddled together in the entrance passages of the snow houses.

Early in the morning, the men went out to the sledges. The shoeing of the runners, which were made of split and polished bone of whale, was covered with a thin sheet of ice. The hunter took some water in his mouth, and allowed it to run slowly over the shoeing. Then he polished it with his mittened hand. After the icing had been made smooth, he turned the sledge right side up.

The harpoon was lashed on, the knife was suspended from the antlers that form the back of the sledge, which are used in steering it through rough ice. The hunters then put the dogs in harness. The light team started down to the beach. During the continued cold weather, the rise and fall of the high tides was forming a broken mass of heavy ice on the beach which, as the winter progressed, was constantly increasing in thickness. A beaten path led down through the broken masses to smooth floe. The sledge sped down, and the hunters went off to the sealing ground. At first the unwilling dogs had to be coaxed to go forward, and even spurred on by cries and by the use of the short handled whip, which the driver handled with skill and accuracy, calling upon the lazy dogs, and hitting them at the same time with the points of the whip. Gradually, the dogs warmed up, and ran along swiftly over the smooth floe. When they reached a part of the ice that was broken up by gales, and in which the uplifted floes were frozen together, the driver had to lift his sledge over the sharp edges and broken masses, and progress was slow and difficult.

Finally the hunting ground was reached. The dogs took the scent of the breathing hole of a seal, and they rushed forward with such speed that the driver could hardly restrain them. At some distance from the hole he succeeded in stopping his team. He tied the dogs to a hummock so that they should not run away and then he inspected the seal hole to see whether it was still being visited by the seal. It was completely covered by snow, and discernible only to the experienced eye. He piled up a few blocks of snow on which he sat down. He laid his harpoon down cautiously, and waited. For hours he remained seated there, waiting for the snorting of the seal. The slightest noise would frighten away the wary animal, and, notwithstanding the intense cold, the hunter could not stir. At last he heard the seal. Cautiously he lifted his harpoon, and sent it down vertically into the snow. It hit the seal which tried in vain to escape. The hunter broke the snow covering of the hole, and hauled the animal upon the ice where, with a swift blow on the head, he killed it. Before he loaded it on his sledge he cut it open, and took out the liver which served him as lunch.

Meanwhile the short day had come to an end! The dogs were harnessed to the sledge, and the hunters returned home. When they arrived, they unloaded the sledge, unharnessed the dogs, and took off the heavy outer clothing. The hunter patted his coat carefully to remove the ice formed by the freezing of his breath. Then he put his coat in the storeroom and entered the house. As soon as he came in he took off his sealskin slippers, bird-skin slippers and stockings, which protected his feet against the cold, and his wife placed them on the rack over the lamp to dry. Then she looked them over and mended them carefully so that they should be ready on the following day.

When all the hunters had come back, those who had brought home no game flocked to the house of one of the successful hunters, who butchered his seal and gave to each man a share to eat in the house, or to take home to his family. They talked over the events of the day until late at night.

This life had been going on quietly for all, without exciting events, when No-tongue's youngest child became ill. The boy refused food and drink, and household remedies did not avail. In her anxiety for the life of her darling, Attina appealed to Pakkak and asked him to find out what ailed the child, and if possible to cure him. Pakkak went to No-tongue's hut. As soon as he came in, the lamps were lowered. He sat down on the bed facing the rear wall of the hut and began his incantation. His body shook violently when he called his protecting spirits to help him. He uttered unintelligible sounds and cries.

Finally his incantation stopped. He addressed himself to Attina and said, "Have you sinned? Have you eaten forbidden food? Have you

done forbidden work? What tabus have you transgressed?" She had asked herself what she might have done to bring about her child's sickness, and she remembered that she had scraped the frost from the window of her house, and that she had eaten seal meat and caribou meat on the same day.

She replied, at once, "I confess! I have scraped frost from the window of my house. I have eaten caribou meat and seal meat on the same day. I have sinned."

Pakkak replied, "It is well, my daughter that you have confessed. Now the evil consequences of your sins are forgiven. The black halo that I saw surrounding your body, and that has affected your child, has disappeared and the boy will soon recover." The lamps were lighted again. The confession of Attina's transgressions had appeased the supernatural powers and therefore the parents hoped for the recovery of their son.

For a while the little boy seemed to improve, but suddenly he suffered a severe relapse, and before the help of Pakkak could be summoned, he died. At once No-tongue prepared to bury the boy. He stuffed his own nostrils with caribou hair to prevent contamination by the exhalation from the corpse. The limbs were tied up with thongs and No-tongue carried his dead child out of the hut and up the hills. There he cut the thongs, and thus released the soul of the child. No-tongue covered the body with a vault of stones, being careful that no stone should weigh on it. He deposited the child's toys and returned home. For three days the whole family stayed in the house. No-tongue did not go out a-hunting. Attina did not clean her lamps. She did not move the caribou skin of the bed. She did not mend any clothing. To transgress these rules would have resulted in new misfortunes.

After four days all the members of the family threw away their clothing which had been contaminated by the breath of the dead child, and it was only with the greatest difficulty that they secured enough skins from their neighbors to make a new set for the whole family. Through the charity of friends they were finally provided for.

The death of the child, and the cares of the family weighed heavily on the mind of Petrel, No-tongue's mother. He himself was lighthearted and consoled himself with the thought that they might have other children in the future; but she was an old woman, and felt that she could not carry the burden of her years much longer. She loved her son and her grandchildren, and the thought haunted her mind that she might die in the hut, and that they might be compelled to throw away another set of winter clothing and be exposed to the hardships of the winter without adequate protection. If only she could die away from home, and thus spare her dear ones the consequences of another sickness and death. The thought preyed on her mind and finally she resolved to end her own life.

The long Arctic night had set in, and only at noon came the sun near enough to the horizon to spread the faint light of dawn over the ice and mountains. One night when it was bitterly cold and the snow was drifting, lashed by a strong wind, old Petrel left the house and walked across the ice to a small island. There in a nook of barren rocks she piled up a wall of stones, and sat down behind it, in order to allow herself to freeze to death. Her thoughts dwelled with her children, and she was satisfied that she was not going to die of sickness in her bed, for then her future life would have been one of agony and torture in the lower world where there is only want and famine, where cold and struggle prevail all the year round. By choosing her own death she looked forward to a happy life in the upper world. There she was going to play ball, and her friends would see her joyful motions in the rays of the Aurora Borealis. She would enjoy comfort and plenty and the cares of this world, as well as the tortures of the lower world would be spared her. Her limbs became numb with the cold and she went to sleep, her mind filled with pleasant visions.

During the night Attina roused herself to trim her lamp. She chanced to look about, and noticed that Petrel was not there. She called her husband who at once guessed what had happened. He gave the alarm and soon all the sledges were out. No tracks were to be seen in the drifting snow, and the whole party scattered in different directions to search for the old woman. To right and left along the coast, north and south they went on their sledges. Usuk, the bachelor, who did menial work for Pakkak, had joined the party. He, the despised and ridiculed one, found the old woman in time to save her from death. Notwithstanding her resistance, he carried her to his sledge, and hurried home. She was taken into the house, covered with a warm blanket and scolded for the unnecessary worry that she had given to her family and to her neighbors. She was ill-satisfied with her rescue, but submitted to the friendly influence of her light-hearted son.

It seemed that with this event the ill luck of No-tongue had spent itself, and the rest of the winter passed quietly. The weather was propitious and no long continued gales kept the hunters at home. The snow was hard and crisp so that the hunting ground could be reached without difficulty. Early in February, the first rays of the sun struck the high mountains and although the cold was still intense, the daylight made hunting and work easier. Now and then visitors came in from distant villages to see their relatives. Everybody flocked to the hut where they were visiting, to hear the news. There was much to tell about success in hunting, about marriage and birth, sickness and death. For months, the village had been cut off from all intercourse with the outside world, because the strong currents that washed the foot of the promontories prevented the formation of ice, and only after the cold had continued long enough, was the sea covered by a continuous floe, which allowed the villagers to travel unhampered from place to place.

One day a number of travelers were discovered, whose sledge, dogs and gait did not seem familiar. The news spread rapidly through the village and the women and children assembled on a point of vantage, straining their eyes in an attempt to discover who the visitors were. Soon, Pakkak recognized an old friend who lived many days' journey away, and whom he had not seen for many years. He shouted, "There is Eiderduck." When the women knew that the visitors were friends of Pakkak, they burst forth in song and laughter. They waved their arms and jumped about. The frightened children hid, crying, behind their mothers. Most of the men went down to the ground ice to meet the strangers, and to help them to unload their sledges. Pakkak led Eiderduck and his companions to a snow house, and treated them hospitably with frozen seal meat.

While they were eating, the people crowded into the house. They sat on the bed platform, and squatted on the floor until there was no more room. Those who could not get into the house crouched in the entrance to get a glimpse of the visitors, and to hear what they had to say. All the older people had some friends in the villages through which the travelers had passed, and therefore their reports were listened to with keenest interest, interest which communicated itself to the younger generation, who thus learned about the family relationships and the history of all the people who lived many miles up and down the coast line.

One of the saddest stories that Eiderduck had to tell was that of some people who had been caribou hunting in the fjord Muddy Water. In the fall, when they were preparing to move camp, the frost set in very suddenly, covering the sea with ice. Heavy snows fell in calm weather. The sledges and the dogs sank deeply into the soft snow so that the people were practically unable to move. Soon they were starving. Many died. In one house lived an old woman with her three sons and a daughter. Her oldest son, Powlak, decided to go to the neighboring village to seek aid of the people. He left his only surviving dog with his mother, that she might use it for food after he was gone. Then he started on his dangerous tramp through the soft snow.

A short time after Powlak had left, his mother missed the dog. She went in search of it, and found that its footprints led to one of the neighboring huts and did not come out again. For some time no sound had been heard in that hut. She thought that the people were dead and she had avoided going in. Now, however, when she needed the dog, she overcame her fear. She called in through the entrance and found that the people were alive, although hardly able to stir. She asked, "Is my dog here?" The house owner denied that it was there, saying that she had not seen it. The old woman, however, searched, and finally when she lifted the heather on the bed she found its skinned body. She became very angry and took the meat. The people were so weak and famished that they could not resist. She took the dog home and she and her children lived on it. Her neighbors soon died of exhaustion. The pangs of hunger had so hardened Powlak's mother, at other times a kind-hearted woman, that she only thought of her own salvation, and felt no pity for the sufferings of others.

When Powlak reached the neighboring village, he found that the people had caught two whales in the fall of the preceding year. He told them that the people in Muddy Water were starving—that a few had tried to reach other places, but that they must have perished in the attempt, since nothing had been heard from them. Powlak's friends were very kind to him. They gave him food to eat and for a few days they did not let him return to his starving mother. They said to him, "Stay here. Why do you want to perish? Your mother, your brothers and your sister are certainly dead by this time." Powlak, however, said, "I am sure they are alive." When he insisted on returning as soon as he had recuperated, his friends

gave him an old dog and a whale-bone toboggan which they loaded with whale meat, skin and blubber. He started on his way back.

When he reached his home after untold difficulties, he went to the window of his mother's hut and asked, standing outside, "Are you all dead?" His mother replied, "There is life in us yet." Then he went in, gave them the whale meat and whale skin, and learned of what had happened during his absence. The food which he had obtained gave him the strength to go out, and he had the good fortune to find a seal hole and as the season progressed, conditions became better and he was able to supply his family with food and clothing. A great number of the villagers, however, had starved to death....

It was late in the night when the crowd began to dwindle leaving Eiderduck and the other visitors to sleep.

As the season progressed and the sun rose, the seals whelped. The skin of the young seal is white and wooly and highly prized for warm clothing. Therefore, the whole village set out to hunt for them. The dogs take the scent of the seal hole, and the poor pup is dragged out with a hook and the hunter kills it by stepping on it.

One day when Pakkak was out hunting young seals, he found himself suddenly confronted by a great polar bear, which was also out in pursuit of seals. He always made it a point to raise good hunting dogs, and the large wolf-like gray creatures were eager to attack the bear which tried to escape. Pakkak never hesitated when there was a chance to get a bear. He cut the traces of two of his strongest dogs, which ran in pursuit. When the bear saw that the dogs were about to overtake him, it climbed an iceberg and took its position on a narrow ledge where its back was protected by the sheer ice wall. It sat up on its haunches. The dogs scrambled up the slippery ice, and when Pakkak saw that they held the bear at bay, he cut the traces of the others, jumped off the sledge, and approached lance in hand. His knife was hanging in its scabbard at his side.

The bear defended itself with its paws and teeth, and already one of the dogs lay bleeding on the ice. The bear, however, could not move on account of the swift attacks of the dogs. Pakkak approached fearlessly. With a swift throw he tried to pierce the bear's heart.

His position was dangerous. The bear held the ledge, and by a single movement of its forelegs might throw the hunter down the steep side of the iceberg. With a swing of its powerful forelegs, it broke the lance. If Pakkak had not jumped back, he might have been caught in the embrace of the bear. There was nothing to do now, but attack the bear with the long hunting knife. He approached again, and watched until the bear, turning to the worrying dogs, exposed its side. Then with a powerful stroke, Pakkak stabbed it in the side. However, he was not quick enough, and, with its claws, the bear tore a deep gash in his shoulder. Then it rolled over, and fell down to the ice floe.

Without paying any attention to his wound, Pakkak skinned the bear and butchered it and rolled it on the sledge. He spliced the traces of the dogs and turned back home where his success was greeted with joy.

Then Pakkak tied the bladder and gall of the bear, together with his drill, to the tip of his spear which he put upright in the ground in front of his house. By this rite, the bear's soul which remains for three days with the body, must be appeased.

The people asked Pakkak about his wound and his battle with the bear. He scoffed at the danger in which he had been pretending that to kill a fierce bear was to him no more of a task than to harpoon a harmless seal. His wife tended his wound, which was so deep that it took weeks to heal.

One day, No-tongue had been out sealing with Pakkak's brother, Ikeraping. As luck would have it he was very successful, while Ikeraping, the strong and skillful hunter, had not killed a single seal. This annoyed Ikeraping, who was ashamed to go home without game. Therefore, he demanded of No-tongue that he should give up his seals to him. No-tongue refused, but Ikeraping became so furious and aggressive that No-tongue, who was by nature timid, gave way and let him have what he wanted. The injustice, however, rankled in No-tongue's mind. It was not the first time that Ikeraping had lorded it over No-tongue, and No-tongue was afraid that sometime, in a quarrel with Ikeraping, he might be killed. Notongue talked the matter over with the other people, but they were all too much afraid of Ikeraping and Pakkak and their brothers, to venture to do away with the aggressive Ikeraping.

Now No-tongue was prompted to leave the village in which he had spent many years. For a long time he had been talking of the distant home from which he had come with his mother, when he was a very young man. At that time he wanted to see the world, and he had drift-

ed from village to village along the whole coast line until finally he had settled down with his wife. The memory of his old home had never left him, and he longed to go back and see his relatives and the scenes of his childhood. The quarrel with Ikeraping strengthened his decision to leave this year, despite the ties which held him to the village where his children were born and were growing up. Although the feeding of many dogs was a burden, on account of the large amount of meat they demanded, No-tongue had strengthened his dog team by raising a number of pups. He had now an excellent team of ten dogs. His sledge was in good repair. And so, before the melting of the snow made traveling difficult, No-tongue was determined to depart. His wife would accompany him into the distant country which, to her, was a foreign land. It would take several years to accomplish the journey.

The departure of No-tongue was the beginning of the breaking up of the winter village. The families were already planning for the summer hunt. Soon, the brooks would be running. The walrus would come near the shore. Whales would come blowing in the open water. Salmon would ascend the rivers. Young geese would be plentiful, and the caribou would come back. The time of happiness was approaching of which No-tongue once sang:

Ayaya, beautiful is the great world when summer is coming at last!
Ayaya, beautiful is the great world when the caribou begin to come!
Ayaya, when the little brooks roar in our country.
Ayaya, I feel sorry for the gulls, for they cannot speak,
Ayaya, I feel sorry for the ravens, for they cannot speak.
Ayaya, if I cannot catch birds I quickly get plenty of fish.
Ayaya!

Franz Boas

Picture credits

Bridgeman Images: 133

British Museum: 138

Library of Congress: 10, 13, 16, 18, 21, 26, 29, 30, 36, 40, 44, 47, 48, 51, 52, 55, 64, 72, 75, 81, 84, 87, 94, 104, 107, 110, 114, 116, 119, 125, 127, 135, 143, 144, 147, 150, 153, 165, 169, 170, 173, 175, 176, 181, 184, 187, 190

National Archives and Records Administration, USA: 157

Wellcome Collection: 34, 60, 82, 93

Wikimedia Commons: 25, 43, 59, 63, 69, 76, 78, 89, 91, 97, 98, 103, 108, 111, 122, 130